26

THE GIRLS
OF CANBY HALL

HELP
WANTED!

EMILY CHASE

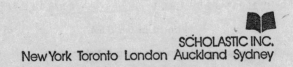

SCHOLASTIC INC.

New York Toronto London Auckland Sydney

ISBN 0-590-41371-6

12 11 10 9 8 7 6 5 4 3 2 1   8 9/8 0 1 2 3/9

Printed in the U.S.A.   01

First Scholastic printing, February 1988

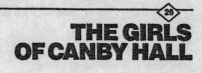

**THE GIRLS
OF CANBY HALL**

26

**HELP
WANTED!**

THE GIRLS
OF CANBY HALL

CHAPTER ONE

It was four o'clock in the afternoon as October Houston, a newspaper tucked under one arm, strode across the campus of Canby Hall, a girls' boarding school in Massachusetts. Four in the afternoon, she thought, and the place is almost as empty as the Texas range right before a tornado hits.

It was a perfect day, too — warm, sunny, breezy, and bright, the kind of day that usually sent the girls of Canby Hall streaming from the dormitories, heading for the tennis courts, the softball field, the lake, anyplace but indoors. Yet except for a few girls making quick dashes back and forth between Baker, Charles, and Addison Houses, Toby practically had the entire campus to herself.

Smiling as she bounded through the front doors of Baker House, Toby knew the reason: Today, all the action was indoors. Throughout the three dormitories, girls were carting dusty suitcases up from the basements, pulling winter clothes from the backs of the closets, searching under beds for missing shoes, and exchanging addresses and phone numbers. School was over and it was time to go home.

Taking the stairs two at a time, Toby made her way to the fourth floor, where most of the rooms were starting to look the way they had in the fall, when school had opened. Without the pictures and posters girls had put up on the walls and the brightly-colored throw-rugs, the rooms were quickly losing their personalities.

In Room 407, though, which was Toby's room, nothing had changed. Her roommate Jane Barrett's corner still had its tasteful Bostonian decorations — a soft, blue-gray rug and an antique quilt; her other roommate Andrea Cord's collection of stuffed animals still sat on top of her bold geometric-print bedspread; and Toby still hadn't packed the photograph of her horse, Max, or untaped the tea bag that dangled from the ceiling above her bed. Far from fading away, the three very different personalities that occupied Room 407 were there in full force.

It felt a little weird not to be packing along with everyone else, Toby thought. Of course, in a month, she and Jane and Andy would be leaving, too, heading for home themselves. But for the first month of vacation, the three of them were staying right there in Baker House. They'd sleep in the dorm, eat in the town of Greenleaf, and as Andy had put it, "be our own bosses for a while."

Of course, they weren't going to be completely alone. Maggie Morrison and Dee Adams from down the hall would be there. They both had jobs in the library and were going to use the money they earned to help pay for the next year's tuition. And Penny Vanderark, whose parents were on a cruise, was also staying for a few weeks.

They weren't exactly going to be their own bosses, either. Nobody's parents would have agreed to that, not even Toby's father, who let her ride the range alone from dawn to dusk. But staying in a town, even a quiet town like Greenleaf, was different, so they were lucky that Meredith Pembroke, Baker's housemother, had decided to work in the dean's office and would be on campus for most of the summer.

Still, they'd be almost on their own, and Toby thought it was going to be great. All they had to do now was find jobs. Toby and Andy could both use the money, and even though Jane probably had enough money to retire now, at the age of fifteen, she thought that being a "career girl" for a month would be an interesting experience.

"Here it is!" Toby cried, going into 407

and waving the newspaper. "Hot off the press. Let's hope we find something."

"Of course we will," Jane said, looking up from the letter she was writing to her parents. "There can't be that much competition for jobs in Greenleaf."

"Right." Andy, a pretty black girl, nodded enthusiastically. "And we're all young, and bright, and ready to work. Who could resist us?"

Laughing, the three roommates divided up the Help Wanted section of the Greenleaf newspaper and settled onto their beds to study the ads. For ten minutes, the room was completely silent. Then Toby looked up. "Could somebody translate this for me?" Running her hand through her curly, red hair, she cleared her throat, and read, " 'WP Op for Mktg firm. Must have Wang exp. Excel pot'l & perks.' " Toby looked at her two roommates, her green eyes mystified. "What in thunderation does that mean?"

"I think I can figure some of it out," Andy said. "Pot'l means potential and perks means getting something besides a paycheck — like a company car or an expense account for lunches."

Toby grinned. "Sounds great. Now if I could just figure out what the job is, I'd go for it."

Jane shook her head. "Forget it," she advised. "A Wang is a kind of computer, and a

WP Op means a word processor operator."
Stepping across the room, she peered over
Toby's shoulder at the ad. "A marketing
firm wants to hire somebody who's experi-
enced in operating a Wang computer."

"You're right, I'd better forget it," Toby
agreed. "I don't know much about computers,
and I don't know anything about marketing."

"Here's something I might be interested
in," Jane said, her long blonde hair brushing
the newspaper as she leaned over it. " 'Jr.
Secy.' That's a junior secretary, I guess. 'Heavy
phones.' "

"Heavy phones?" Andy said. "What do they
want you to do, carry fifty of them at a time?"

"I think it means it's a busy office and the
secretary has to answer the phones a lot," Jane
explained.

"Well that doesn't sound too hard," Andy
said. "What else does it say?"

Jane read on. " 'Must be bright, personable,
super-organized, able to. . . .' "

Andy's eyes lit up and Toby's mouth curved
into a big smile. The two of them tried not to
look at each other, but they couldn't help it.
As soon as their eyes met, they burst out
laughing.

"What's so funny?" Jane stopped reading.

For an answer, Andy pointed to Jane's desk,
on which a lopsided pile of books teetered at
the edge, three empty soda cans stood next to
the empty pencil cup, and assorted pieces of

clothing were scattered. "Did you say 'super-organized'?" she asked.

Jane started to frown, but finally she couldn't help laughing along with them. "All right, it's true, I'm not the most organized person in the world," she admitted. "Maybe you ought to go after this one, Andy. After all, your side of the room always looks like a display in a furniture store window."

Andy laughed again, but shook her head. "I could probably organize an office, but look — it says able to handle bookkeeping. I don't know how to do that."

"But how hard can that be?" Jane said, whose wealthy Boston upbringing included lessons in social etiquette and ballroom dancing, and such basics as handling large sums of money.

"Come on," Andy said. "How many junior secretaries do you know who can do book-keeping?"

"I only know one *secretary*," Jane told her. "My father's."

"And she does bookkeeping?"

"No," Jane said. "*He* types, and speaks a couple of languages. But I see your point. I guess neither one of us would make a good jr. secy."

"I wouldn't either, that's for sure," Toby said. "Even if I could type, I'd feel trapped behind a desk. I'd have a bad case of cabin fever in about ten seconds flat."

"Okay, we'll forget about that one." Jane sighed. "It's too bad. The ad says it's an excel oppty."

Toby nodded. "And it had great pot'l, too."

"Opptee? Potle?" Meredith, a tall young woman with dark hair and a friendly smile stuck her head around the door. Waving a clipboard, she said, "I was just doing some inventory in the empty rooms, and I couldn't help overhearing you. What kind of language are you three speaking?"

"The language of the jobhunter," Jane explained, pointing to the newspaper. "We're trying to find something with great opportunity and terrific potential."

"Actually, we're just trying to find something we can *do*," Andy said.

Tucking the clipboard underneath her arm, Meredith leaned against the doorframe for a moment. "Well, what *can* you do?" she asked.

The three of them thought about it. Andy had helped out at her parents' restaurant in Chicago, and Toby had earned money doing chores on the ranch. Jane's closest brush with employment was helping her mother plan the decorations for a charity ball. Those things, along with the time the roommates worked in the Cords' restaurant over Christmas vacation, hardly qualified as substantial work experience.

"I guess mending fences and cleaning horse

stalls isn't going to impress anybody here in the East," Toby admitted.

"It impressed Randy Crowell," Andy reminded her. The Crowells owned a horse farm not too far from Canby Hall, and twenty-year-old Randy was the first boy Toby had ever had a crush on. That was over now. In fact, Toby was having a long-distance romance with Neal Worthington, who lived in Boston. But Toby and Randy were great friends, and whenever Toby needed an escape from the crowds at school, she was always welcome at the farm. "I bet Randy's dad would hire you," Andy went on.

"I thought of that," Toby told her. "But it was too late by the time I asked. They've already got all the summer hands they need." She thought a minute. "I'd really like to do something outdoors. Maybe I could mow lawns."

"Well, I've done a lot of baby-sitting," Andy said. "Maybe somebody needs a mother's helper."

"Don't get me wrong," Meredith told them, "but I think you're going at this backward. Sure, it would be great if you could get exactly the kind of job you want. But I don't think you should be too picky about it."

"You mean we should take what we can get," Andy said.

"I think you might have to," Meredith agreed. Straightening up, she started to go, but then stopped. "And don't bother with jobs that talk about potle," she said with a grin. "You're not looking for potential. You're looking for temporary work for a month."

"She's right," Andy said after Meredith had left. "We're looking at the wrong ads. We don't want to be junior secys and WP Ops. Come on, there's got to be a temporary or summer job section in here."

Determined to find something, they all turned back to the newspaper. Unfortunately, the list of temporary jobs was short. Greenleaf was a small town, and besides, it was so close to summer that most of the jobs had already been taken. When they finally stopped looking and headed downstairs for their last meal in the dining hall, the roommates had only found two ads that seemed promising. One was for a dogwalker, which Toby was sure she could handle. The other was for assistant captain at the Greenleaf Inn, the town's best restaurant. Andy planned to go after that one.

"After all," she said as they got in line in the dining hall, "I know the restaurant business. An assistant captain is sort of the head busboy and back-up host. I bet I could do the job with my eyes closed."

"I don't think the customers would like that much," Jane remarked dryly. Then, looking at the grayish, retangular slab of meatloaf on her plate, she shuddered. "I wish we were having dinner there right now."

"Somehow I don't think we'll be eating in that place very much," Toby said. "Not unless we get lucky and find jobs that pay a mint."

"Hey, just think!" Andy said. "If I do get the job there, I'll get free meals while I'm on duty."

"That's right, so just be sure to bring home a doggie bag," Toby reminded her.

As they sat down to eat, Dee, Maggie, and Penny joined them, and the "Baker House Leftovers," as they called themselves, discussed being on their own.

"I'm a little nervous about it," Maggie confessed, pushing her glasses up on her nose. "I mean, it's going to be so weird after tomorrow, when everyone else is gone. Baker House is going to seem like an abandoned building, with all those empty rooms."

"It'll be terrific." Dee, who was from California and very independent, looked at her roommate and grinned. "Just think, no waiting in line for a shower. No hearing somebody else's music at three in the morning. Nobody shouting at us to turn *our* music down." Swinging her straight blonde hair off her shoulder, she laughed. "And, since we're only working from nine to two, we'll have almost the whole afternoon free. I just wish we were closer to the ocean."

Maggie laughed, too, her brown eyes crinkling. "Well, you could always try to surf in the wishing pond," she suggested, mentioning the small pond where students threw pennies and wished for good grades and nice-looking boys.

"You do that," Penny said, in her lilting Georgia accent, "and I'll just have to write a story about it. In fact, I think I'll take notes on this whole next month and then write it up for next year's literary magazine. I have a feeling our stay here is going to be chock-full of surprises."

CHAPTER TWO

Andy's alarm went off at seven-thirty the next morning, and she caught it before it had even stopped buzzing. Pushing back the sheet, she swung her legs over the side of the bed, stood up, and started in on some leg stretches. She had a dancer's body; in fact, her goal was to someday be a professional ballerina, and she made early-morning exercises look as graceful and natural as walking.

But dancing wasn't on Andy's mind that morning. Getting a job was. The Greenleaf Inn was going to start interviewing people at nine, and she wanted to be there first. If you make a good enough impression, she told herself, maybe they won't bother seeing anybody else.

It was very important to Andy to get a job, and to get one fast. Her parents hadn't been exactly thrilled at the idea of her staying on at Canby Hall after almost everyone else had left. It was when she'd told them she wanted to work and help out with her school expenses that they'd finally given in. They said it was a very responsible, thoughtful thing to do, and they'd been proud of her for thinking of it.

If she didn't get a job, though, Andy knew there was no way they'd let her stay. And she wanted to stay. She knew any money she earned would be appreciated. And it wasn't that she didn't love her parents, her two brothers, and her baby sister; they were a great family and really close. It was just that sometimes they were a little *too* close, and as much as she loved them, she thought it was important to let them know that she could stand on her own two feet. Getting this job would make everything perfect.

Finished with her exercises, Andy slipped on a short, orange cotton robe, and grabbed a fluffy white towel. She was halfway to the door when a sound made her stop and turn around.

Jane, her blonde hair tangled and half-covering her face, had reached for her clock and knocked it to the floor. Her eyes still closed, she was fumbling around, trying to find it. "Time is it?" she mumbled sleepily.

Laughing, Andy picked up the clock and placed it in Jane's hand. "I hate to tell you this, but it's only a quarter to eight."

"In the morning?" Jane's voice was groggy

but outraged. "What are you doing up?
School's over."

"I'm trying to get a job," Andy said. "Remember? We're all going to get jobs and work
for a while?"

"Mmm. I suppose Toby's already gone."

"Up at dawn, as usual," Andy said, heading
for the door again. "I know how you hate
mornings," she called back over her shoulder,
"but that's when most people go to work.
Maybe you ought to get up and get used to it."

After Andy had left for the shower, Jane
snuggled back down in her bed. In her
opinion, the only civilized thing to do at
seven forty-five in the morning was sleep. Of
course, she wanted to get a job, too, but there
had to be jobs that started later than eight.
Eleven, she thought, beginning to doze again,
eleven would be perfect. That would give her
time for the kind of long, leisurely breakfast
that she loved.

At the thought of breakfast, Jane's stomach
woke up. Sleepiness and hunger fought a
quick battle, and hunger won. By the time
Andy came back to dress, Jane was actually
sitting up.

"I don't believe it," Andy joked. "Was
there a major earthquake?"

"Just some major hunger pangs," Jane said.
"I thought I'd have breakfast at The Greaf
and look at the want-ads while I'm there."

The Greaf (originally Greenleaf, but the sign was missing some letters) Diner served great breakfasts. It also had a great-looking counterboy named Cary Slade, who happened to be Jane's boyfriend. "That sounds like a good idea," Andy said with a grin. "And who knows? Maybe they're hiring."

Jane smiled. "I already thought of that, but they're not. Cary said he was lucky they kept him on. Summers must be awfully slow around here."

"Not this summer," Andy said, putting on a dark blue skirt and an apricot blouse that she thought was a good outfit for a job interview. "As long as we're here, Greenleaf's going to be hopping!"

After Andy left, Jane showered, dressed, and left the dorm. The campus was busy this morning, as parents helped daughters pile suitcases and boxes and bicycles into cars. Patrice Allardyce, the school's cool, elegant headmistress, mingled with the families, shaking hands and chatting. A lot of the girls had left the day before and the rest were leaving today. By tonight, Jane thought, Canby Hall will be a ghost town.

Leaving the crowds and the campus behind, Jane walked along a quiet, shaded street into the town of Greenleaf. In ten minutes, she was at The Greaf, and the minute Cary saw her, he broke into a big smile.

"You're awake!" he said, pretending to be shocked. "Your eyes are open! Quick, somebody pinch me. I must be dreaming!"

Several heads turned toward Jane as she walked to the counter and sat down. "Can't you just say good morning?" she asked, burying her face in a menu.

"Sure I can, but it wouldn't be half as much fun as watching you blush," Cary said, his blue eyes twinkling. Even though he was as much a Boston blue blood as Jane, with the same patrician background, no one would ever have guessed. Cary was so casual and outgoing that most people warmed up to him immediately, while getting to know Jane was an "uphill battle," as Toby put it. A student at Oakley Prep, a boy's school down the road from Canby Hall, and the lead guitarist in a rock band known as Ambulance, Cary Slade was crazy about Jane, but that didn't stop him from teasing her. "What got you up so early, anyway?" he asked, wiping the counter with a damp cloth. "An earthquake?"

"You sound like Andy." Jane yawned and put down the menu. "First I'd like some coffee, and then orange juice, pancakes, and bacon. Then I'll be able to communicate."

Halfway through her stack of syrup-drenched pancakes, Jane discovered that she was awake enough to talk. "Is the morning paper here yet?" she asked.

"Yet?" Cary laughed. "It's been here since

we opened two hours ago. It's usually sold out by now." Raising himself on tiptoe, he looked toward the cash register. "Wait, there's one copy left." Setting down the coffeepot, he dashed out from behind the counter, snatched up the paper, and sped back, presenting it to Jane with a flourish.

"Now I get it," he said, as Jane turned to the Help Wanted section. "You're up so bright and early because you want to get a jump on all the other job-seekers."

"That's right," Jane said, scanning the listings for temporary jobs. "There's nothing new in here," she complained after a minute. "This is the same as yesterday."

"I'm not surprised," Cary said. "After all, Greenleaf isn't Boston or New York. You're just not going to find hundreds of jobs up for grabs."

"But there has to be something," Jane protested. "Dee and Maggie found work, and Andy and Toby are out answering ads right now. I can't be the only one who's not qualified."

Cary wasn't sure what to say. He knew Jane was smart and could work as hard as anyone. But what kind of work? Even if there had been an opening at The Greaf, they probably wouldn't have hired her. They would have taken one look at her and decided she wasn't the type to wait tables. In fact, most people would have the same reaction.

With her background, her Boston accent, and her preppy clothes, Jane just didn't look cut out for any kind of work, especially summer-type work like painting houses or taking somebody's little kids to the playground.

The diner was quiet at the moment, so Cary finished wiping the counter and came around to the other side. Taking the stool next to Jane's, he peered at the paper. She was right, there wasn't much to choose from.

Then, a small ad caught his eye. "Look at this," he said, pointing to it. " 'Cadwell Employment Agency. Serving Greenleaf and surrounding areas since 1960. Let us find the job that's right for you.' "

"I didn't see that yesterday," Jane said, reading the ad again. "You know, this could be exactly what I need. They probably have lots of jobs that I haven't even thought of. And once they interview me, they'll know exactly where to send me. Just think," she went on excitedly, "I might have a job before the day's over."

"It's worth a try, that's for sure." Seeing a new customer come in, Cary slid off the stool and went back behind the counter. "And listen, if it doesn't work out, I could always use somebody to tune my guitar for me. I'll even pay the minimum wage."

Jane laughed. She could no more tune a guitar than she could play one, and Cary knew it. But with the Cadwell Employment

Agency on her side, it didn't matter. She was sure they'd find something for her, something just right. After all, that was their business.

An employment agency, she thought, tearing out the ad and putting it in her purse. Now that's a civilized way to find a job.

While Jane was hurrying back to Baker House to change her shorts for a skirt, Toby was walking up to the door of what she already called the "Dog House."

There was no sign of dogs at the small yellow house, but Toby knew they were there. When she'd called earlier she'd heard them barking in the background, and the woman she'd spoken to was constantly telling them to hush. There were five of them, the woman had said, and they needed walking morning and evening. They also needed grooming twice a week, and that was at least a three-hour job. They spent most of the time in the backyard, so it needed cleaning daily.

The woman was getting older, she'd said, and she had arthritis and couldn't take good care of the dogs anymore. She wanted someone young and strong for the job, and she wasn't sure a girl would be right. But after Toby gave her a quick run-down of her life on the ranch — exercising and washing horses, cleaning stalls, and herding cattle — the woman had agreed to see her.

As Toby stepped up to the front door, she

could hear birds chirping and somebody's lawn mower droning in the distance, but otherwise, everything seemed quiet and peaceful. Her hopes high, she reached out and pushed the doorbell.

Immediately, there was an explosion of noise. Even though the door was closed, Toby stepped back from it as she heard the wild howling and yapping from inside the house. She took another step back as what sounded like a herd of wild beasts threw their bodies against the door, scraping the wood with their nails, and whining to get at the prey on the other side. The prey, Toby thought, that's me.

The scratching and yowling went on for a full minute, while Toby reminded herself that she'd never been afraid of any animal in her life. At least, not any domesticated animal. Unfortunately, these dogs — they had to be dogs, the woman hadn't said anything about a pack of wolves — didn't sound anywhere near domesticated.

Finally, Toby heard a human voice on the other side of the door. "Back!" a woman shouted, "Get down! Mind your manners before the neighbors start to complain!"

The wild barking gradually stopped, but the dogs replaced it with whines and deep-throated growls, which didn't sound any less threatening to Toby. She stood very still as she heard a chain being unlatched and saw the door start to swing open.

The open door brought the dogs back to life, and they leaped up in full force. Toby was glad there was a screen door between them, but she had her doubts about how long it would last.

Two of the dogs looked like German shepherds, one was definitely a Doberman, and the other two were mixtures. Mixtures of what, Toby wasn't sure, except that they were big. They were *all* big.

Just behind this group of fierce-looking canines, Toby spotted a small, grey-haired woman with a round, wrinkled face and a sweet smile. She looked like she weighed about ninety pounds, and Toby decided it wasn't her arthritis that kept her from handling the dogs, it was just that she was outnumbered by about four and a half to one.

"Mornin'," Toby called out. "My name's Toby Houston. I talked to you earlier?"

"Now hush!" the woman said, and then smiled at Toby again. "I'm Cora Walters, and I wasn't hushing *you*, of course. I was talking to my babies."

Some babies, Toby thought.

"Come in, come in!" Mrs. Walters called over the barking. "Don't be nervous. These boys are just frisky, that's all. They won't bite unless I tell them to."

Hoping she seemed calm and relaxed, Toby pushed open the screen door and stepped inside. The dogs immediately surrounded her, sniffing her hands and boots, and tripping all over themselves trying to get closer to her.

One of the German shepherds, satisfied that she wasn't going to rob the house, jumped up, put his front paws on Toby's shoulders, and barked in her face.

"That's Charlie," Mrs. Walters told her. "He's saying hello."

"Hello, Charlie," Toby said, nervously. Charlie barked again.

"Charlie, get down!" Mrs. Walters ordered. Charlie didn't move. "Just push him away," she told Toby. "He's got the worst manners of them all."

Toby pushed tentatively, and Charlie responded with a rumble from somewhere deep in his chest. Toby looked at Mrs. Walters, but the woman was already leading the way down the hall toward the back door. "Charlie, down," Toby commanded. Another rumble. Toby said it again, and this time Charlie got down, most of his weight landing on Toby's left foot. But Toby knew he wasn't minding her — the other dogs were heading down the hall, and Charlie had decided he didn't want to be left out.

Well, neither do I, Toby thought, following him. There's not a dog on this earth I can't handle, and as long as Charlie doesn't bite, I can teach him a thing or two about manners.

Out in the big backyard, which was enclosed by a seven-foot-high chain-link fence, Mrs.

Walters turned to Toby. "As I said, I'm getting too old to look after my babies properly. They're good boys, they just need a strong hand sometimes."

Toby nodded, not sure how good a boy Charlie was.

"You're awfully slender," Mrs. Walters said, looking Toby up and down. "Are you sure they won't be too much for you? That's the important thing. I can't have them getting loose and running wild, or my neighbors would call the police, and I might have to give them up."

"Yes, ma'am, I'm sure," Toby told her. "I'm skinny, but I'm strong. And like I told you, I've been around animals all my life."

"Well, that's it then," Mrs. Walters said. "If I have you for a month, then that will give me time to find someone permanent. Come on, I'll show you where their leashes are."

"You mean you want me to start now?" Toby asked.

"Of course. It's way past time for their walk."

So Toby, with the five dogs hot on her heels, went to get the leashes and begin her first day on the job.

CHAPTER THREE

Just about the time that Toby was setting out with Mrs. Walters' dogs, Andy was being called for her interview at the Greenleaf Inn.

Finally, she thought, clutching her application and following the manager out of the room. She'd arrived at the inn half an hour before the ad said they'd start the interviews, and she'd expected to be the first. Instead, she was the thirteenth.

Telling herself not to be superstitious, she'd gotten an application form and joined all the other hopeful assistant captains in the small room next to the office. There were only eight chairs, so Andy found an empty space on the wall and leaned against it.

Besides the usual things like name and age, the application wanted to know all about Andy's employment history. Since she was only fifteen, her history was pretty short. In fact, baby-sitting and snow shoveling were the only real jobs she'd ever had. The things she'd done in her parents' restaurant didn't count, because she hadn't been paid.

Fortunately, there was a big blank space at the bottom of the application, and Andy used it to list the work she'd done at the restaurant: waiting on tables, taking reservations, and ordering supplies a few times, and being the hostess for two nights when her mother and father had both come down with the flu. That had been a crazy time, she remembered. It seemed like half of Chicago had picked those two nights to have barbecued ribs, and Dad had been sure the whole place was going to fall apart. But she and her older brother Charles had helped keep it running so smoothly that nobody knew the owners were sick in bed.

Through the open door of the room where she was waiting, Andy could hear the clatter of coffee cups and the murmur of voices as people placed their orders or chatted over plates of omelettes and waffles. The dining room of the Greenleaf Inn was a quiet, pretty place, with white linen tablecloths and fresh rosebuds in cut glass vases. It was Jane's kind of restaurant. Andy liked her restaurants with a little more bounce, but still, it would be a great place to work for a month. And she knew she could do it; that was the best part. As she left the room for her interview, Andy straightened her shoulders and put on a confident smile. She might not have a long employment history, but she knew the restaurant business inside and out.

The manager, a tall man with a drooping mustache, led her into another small room, shook her hand, and motioned for her to sit down while he read her application.

After a few moments, he put the paper down and smiled at her. "Ms. Cord," he said. "I can see by your application that you're acquainted with the running of a restaurant."

"Yes, I am." Andy sat up a little straighter and smiled back. "All that work I listed there at the bottom I did in my parents' restaurant in Chicago. My parents opened it twelve years ago, and it's been going strong ever since."

"I'm glad to hear it," the manager said. "Now, about 'all this work,' as you put it. How many hours a week exactly did you spend working there?"

"Well, I didn't count them," Andy said. "I mean I've waited tables a lot, of course. And I've taken reservations two or three times. And I had to order the supplies once because my mother had laryngitis and couldn't even whisper. Then last year both my parents were sick and my brother and I helped out for two nights."

"I see." The manager glanced at the application and then back at her. "So aside from these emergencies, you really haven't spent much time actually doing management work in a restaurant?"

"I suppose not," Andy admitted. "But I really do know the business. My parents talk about it all the time."

"I'm sure they do," he agreed. "However, you'll have to admit that hearing about it, even waiting tables, is quite different from actually being involved in the day-to-day running of it. And that is what being assistant captain would involve."

"Yes, but I'm still sure I can handle it." The interview wasn't going quite the way Andy had imagined, but she wasn't about to give up. "I spent a lot of time at my parents' restaurant, and I watched them run it."

"But the leap from watching to doing is a big one," the manager said. He gently tapped her application. "I'm sorry, Ms. Cord, but you simply don't have the experience."

"But you only want somebody for a month!" Andy protested. She didn't want to argue, but she was sure this man was wrong. "It would probably only take me a few days to catch on, and then I'd be fine."

"Possibly, but that's a risk we can't take," he told her. "The Greenleaf Inn is a famous, beautifully-run establishment. We have to hire someone who can step in and keep it running smoothly, with no hitches." Smiling again, he stood up. "You ask your mother or father, Ms. Cord. They'll tell you — they wouldn't want any hitches in their restaurant, either."

Andy stood up, too. Obviously, the interview was over. "Well, thank you, anyway," she said.

"Thank you, Ms. Cord," he said. "I appreciate your coming in. And good luck with whatever job you do find."

There wasn't anything more to say, so Andy thanked him and left, tossing her application into a wastepaper basket on the way out. As she walked along in the warm sunshine, she thought about what he'd said, and after she got through being mad, she realized he was right. How many times had her mother said, "When you're running a business, the most important thing is the people you hire?" She remembered her parents discussing and arguing about job applications for days before they finally decided which person to hire.

Admit it, Andy, she told herself, your own parents probably wouldn't hire you for that particular job. Not if they had people with more experience to choose from. Why would anybody take a chance on a fifteen-year-old girl when they didn't have to?

Normally cheerful, Andy felt down in the dumps, and she wished Matt were there. A student at Oakley Prep, Matt was quiet and almost shy, but his brown eyes always lit up at the sight of Andy, and he could make her feel special just by looking at her.

But Matt wasn't there. He had a summer job at home, in Philadelphia, and the best he could do was say he'd try to get to Greenleaf for a couple of days.

If he were here now, Andy thought, what would he say? And she grinned, because she knew the answer: "I don't believe this. Ms. Optimistic forgetting how to smile because she didn't get the first job she went after?"

Walking down the street by herself, Andy laughed out loud. Matt would be right. So what if she wasn't busing tables at the Greenleaf Inn? There were other jobs. All she had to do was go out and find one.

While Andy was giving herself a pep talk, Jane was sitting in the office of the Cadwell Employment Agency, waiting to be interviewed. She had an application form, but after giving her name, age, and occupation — student — she'd left it blank. There really was nothing else to write on it, but that didn't bother her. Just because she couldn't type or file or run a cash register didn't mean she wasn't qualified for something. And Jane was confident that the Cadwell Agency would find the right something.

"Ms. Barrett?"

Jane looked up to see a tall woman of about forty standing in the doorway to an office. Her dark hair was pulled back from her thin face, her lipstick was bright red, and she wore about five bracelets on each arm.

"Yes, I'm Jane Barrett," Jane said, standing up and smoothing the wrinkles out of her beige skirt.

"I'm Agatha Cadwell. Come in."

Jane followed her into the office, handed over her application, and sat down.

It took Agatha Cadwell about ten seconds to read the application. Then she looked at Jane. "You're after temporary work, I take it?"

Jane nodded. "Yes, I'll only be here for another month, so I wouldn't be interested in anything permanent."

"Mmm." Ms. Cadwell put her chin in her hands and her bracelets slid to her elbows, jangling wildly. "Doesn't Canby Hall have a student employment service?"

"Yes, but all those jobs have been filled," Jane explained.

Clink went the bracelets as Ms. Cadwell put her hands down. Still staring at Jane, she asked, "Well, your application is a little short on information. What can you do?"

Jane felt a blush start to creep up her neck. Furious, she told herself she had nothing to be embarrassed about. "I don't have any job experience, really, but I'm a good writer, a good student, and most people think I have good taste — in clothes and decorating and things like that."

"Mmm," Ms. Cadwell said again. "Well,

writing and decorating jobs are pretty scarce in Greenleaf."

Jane was starting to dislike Agatha Cadwell. After all, *finding* jobs was *her* job and so far, she hadn't lifted a finger. In her coolest tone, Jane said, "I was hoping you would be the one to tell me what I can do. That's what an employment agency does, isn't it?"

"We try." Ms. Cadwell was busy with a small file-holder now, her long red fingernails clicking against the cards. "No," she said after a minute, "you wouldn't want this."

"I wouldn't want what?" Jane asked, not liking to be second-guessed.

"It's a five-week stint on the assembly line at an electronics factory fifteen miles out of town. You'd be soldering wires onto the back of a metal plate from seven-thirty in the morning to three-thirty in the afternoon."

People who didn't know Jane very well often thought she was a super snob, and most of them would have bet that she wouldn't set foot in a factory, let alone get her hands dirty working on an assembly line. But Jane wasn't afraid of getting her hands dirty, even though she preferred not to. What bothered her about this job were the hours. Seven-thirty to three-thirty? Eight hours, beginning at the crack of dawn?

Andy warned you, she told herself. But still, there have to be some jobs that don't mean getting up with the birds. There *was* one good thing about this factory job, though. It was for five weeks. Since she only had four, she could turn it down without feeling guilty.

"I'm afraid I won't be here long enough for that," she said. "And transportation would be a problem, too."

Ms. Cadwell was still flipping through her cards, and just nodded her head. "No, they want somebody eighteen for this one," she murmured. "Wait . . . no, you'd need typing and shorthand there. Here's a locker room attendant at a sports' club . . . whoops! It's the men's locker room. Let's see, lifeguard . . . no, you're not qualified; tailor's assistant . . . no. . . ."

As Agatha droned on, Jane felt like she was shrinking in her chair. It was a humiliating experience, having someone describe all the things you couldn't do. Jane wasn't used to feeling useless or humiliated, and she decided she'd had enough of it for one morning.

"Well," she broke in, "it doesn't seem that you have anything for me at the moment." Getting up, she gave Ms. Cadwell a frosty smile. "Why don't I leave my application with you and call in a few days?"

Agatha eyed Jane's almost blank application and smiled, too, with relief. "I think that's a good idea," she said. "But I have to warn you — the outlook isn't exactly rosy."

"Thank you very much." Her mouth in a thin line, Jane nodded and left the office.

Still furious, Jane walked swiftly down the street until she reached The Greaf. Cary will want to know what happened, she thought, wishing she could just hide for a while. You might as well get it over with.

Inside the diner, Jane found both Cary and Andy waiting for her, and over vanilla milk shakes, the two girls described their first job-hunting experiences.

"Well, that doesn't sound so bad," Cary commented cheerfully when they'd finished.

Jane stared at him. "Not so bad?" she asked. "How can you say that? Andy's had loads of restaurant experience and they didn't hire her. And I. . . ."

Cary grinned.

"All right, all right, I know. I don't have any experience at all," Jane admitted. "You don't have to rub it in."

"That's what an elite Boston background will do to you," Cary said, still grinning. "Leave you unemployed at age fifteen."

Jane laughed along with him, but even though she laughed, her chin came up and her blue eyes started to sparkle.

"Uh-oh," Andy said. "I saw that. Whenever you raise your chin that way, it means somebody better look out."

"Don't tell me you're still mad at poor Agatha," Cary said teasingly. "Should I call her and warn her you're out for blood?"

"No, you're right, I shouldn't be mad at

her, even though she did make me feel like a
dope," Jane said. Her chin came up a little
more. "In fact, I think she did me a favor. She
just made me more determined than ever to
find a job."

"So it's 'Look out, Greenleaf'?" Cary asked.

"That's right," Jane said. "I don't like to
be told I can't do something." She thought a
minute and then laughed. "You know, I
didn't used to be like that. I think some of
Toby has rubbed off on me. Telling her 'you
can't' is like waving a red flag in front of a
bull."

Andy sipped the last of her milk shake and
nodded. "Speaking of Toby, I wonder if she
had better luck than we did." As she checked
her watch, her eyes widened. "My gosh, she
must have gotten lucky! It's eleven-thirty. I'll
bet she's out walking those dogs right now."

"Walking the dogs" was not exactly what
Toby would have called it. What really happened was that the dogs had walked Toby. Or
dragged her, to be exact.

From the minute she'd gotten the leashes
on them, which took a good twenty minutes,
the dogs had been in charge. They knew where
Toby was headed — to Bradbury Park — and
they didn't want to waste any time getting
there.

Toby had tried everything she could think
of to make them toe the line. She'd called out

"heel," and slapped her thigh, shouted "no!" in what she hoped was a voice full of authority, and yanked on the leashes so hard she expected the dogs to choke. But they didn't pay any attention to her at all. As far as they were concerned, she was a slowpoke, and she was keeping them from having a good time. Most of them just marched right on, ignoring her completely, but Charlie, who pulled the hardest, turned around and looked at her twice. Both times, Toby saw his lip curl back over his extremely sharp teeth.

When they finally reached Bradbury Park, Toby was sure her arms were two inches longer than when she'd started out. She knew Mrs. Walters wanted her to let the dogs run free for half an hour or so in the small section of the park where this was allowed. Toby was then supposed to throw sticks for them to catch. But Toby wasn't quite ready for that yet. Instead, she found a park bench, which was luckily embedded in cement, tied the leashes to it, and collapsed on it, letting her arms hang limp.

"Mrs. Walters was wrong about you," she muttered to the dogs. "You don't have bad manners. You just don't have any manners at all."

The dogs all stared in the opposite direction, as if they couldn't be bothered listening to her.

"If Mrs. Walters really wanted to do right

by you," Toby went on, "she'd send you to school. One week in a good training school and you'd know what respectable dogs are supposed to act like. You guys are shameful. Why, at home, we have dogs riding the herd with us who wouldn't be caught dead with the likes of you."

"I hate to interrupt," a voice said, "but people are beginning to stare."

Looking around, Toby saw Randy Crowell standing behind the bench, the sun shining on his blond hair and an amused smile in his eyes. As usual, the sight of him made her happy. Oh, she'd gotten over wishing he were fifteen instead of twenty, so he could be her boyfriend. She had Neal now and she liked him . . . a lot. But the things that had made her want Randy for a boyfriend made her keep him as a friend — he was bright and warm and easygoing, and best of all, he loved horses as much as she did.

"I guess I do look pretty foolish," Toby said now. "But these mutts wore me out, and I just had to give 'em a piece of my mind."

Laughing, Randy came around and joined her on the bench. The dogs had been lying down, staring longingly at the wide open grassy park, but now they got up and sniffed his boots and knees.

"They smell hay and horses," Randy said, patting a couple of them on the head. "Where did you get five dogs all of a sudden, anyway?"

"They're my job," Toby said. "As of this morning, I'm an official dog-walker. Meet Sam, Rocky, Morris, Fudge, and Charlie."

At the sound of their names, the dogs perked up their ears. "I thought I was lucky to get the job," Toby went on, ignoring their hopeful looks, "but now I'm not so sure. They're more trouble than a passel of mules."

"Come on, they can't be that bad," Randy said. "They probably just need a good run."

"That's what their owner told me. I'm supposed to let them loose here in the park and play with them." Toby shook her head. "I keep putting it off. I just don't know what they'll do when I let them go. What if they don't come back when I call them? So far, they've minded me about as well as a bunch of unbroken horses."

"Well, listen, I have a little time before I have to get back to the farm," Randy said. "I'll stick around if you want me to. Between the two of us, we ought to be able to handle them."

"Thanks, Randy, that'll be great." Toby looked at the dogs. "Okay, you guys," she said. "I'm turning you loose. But when it's time to go home, I want all five of you back the minute I call, you hear?"

One by one, Toby unhooked the leashes. Once the dogs caught on to what was happening, they barked and whined excitedly, and the minute they were free, they tore off across the grass as if there were a fire at their backs.

After a while, one of them brought a stick for her to throw. Pretty soon, she and Randy were tossing sticks like mad, laughing and having a great time. This is going to work out after all, she thought happily. And it's the best kind of job I could have found, much better than sitting around in some stuffy office, having to talk to people all day long.

When it was time to go, Toby crossed her fingers and called for the dogs to come. Amazingly, four of them came at once, and they stood quietly while she refastened their leashes. The one who didn't come was Charlie.

"Charlie, come on, boy!" Toby called, keeping her voice friendly and relaxed. But Charlie must have been biding his time, just waiting for the right moment to make things difficult. Instead of coming, he trotted farther away, then stopped, turned, and barked at her.

"Charlie, come!" Toby didn't sound so friendly this time, but it didn't matter. Charlie just wasn't going to obey.

"I've got an idea," Randy said. "I'll throw him a stick. He's been bringing them back like he's been trained to do it. So when he does, we'll snap the leash on him before he knows what we're up to."

"Good thinking," Toby said.

"Hey, Charlie, look!" Randy called, waving a stick. When he was sure the dog had seen it, he tossed it through the air. Charlie watched it go and took off after it, the way he'd been doing for the past half hour. But when he got to it, he paused for a second, barked once more in Toby's direction, grabbed the stick in his mouth, and took off like a streak for the hedge that bordered the area for the dogs to run in. When he reached the hedge, he sailed over it like a racehorse, his tail flat out behind him, and the stick still in his mouth.

CHAPTER FOUR

At four-thirty that afternoon, Andy, Jane, Dee, Maggie, and Penny were gathered in Room 407, trying to decide where they should eat dinner that night. They'd eaten in various places in Greenleaf over the past year, but tonight was different — tonight they *had* to eat in Greenleaf. The last of the students had left, the campus was quiet, and the dining hall was shut down for the summer.

"Just think, no more Tuna Surprise," Dee said, slipping off the shoes she'd worn to work at the library and wriggling her toes. "No more prehistoric meat. Beginning tonight, we can eat decent food. I say we celebrate."

"Where?" Maggie asked.

"Pizza Pete's, where else?"

"I'm ready now," Andy said eagerly. "Let's really splurge and get one with the works."

Jane, who had been going over the ads in the afternoon paper, looked up and frowned.

"You know," she said thoughtfully, "I just realized that all this eating out is going to cost money. We'll have to be careful, or we'll wind up eating our savings."

"I don't see why *you're* worried about it," Dee commented. After not being able to stand each other, Dee and Jane had finally become friends. But Dee still thought Jane was too privileged for her own good, and she never let her get away with phony remarks like having to watch how much money she spent. "That allowance you get from your parents would probably feed all of us for a month."

"Yes, my family is very generous," Jane agreed calmly. "But when I told them I was going to work, I asked them to stop the allowance as soon as I got a job."

"Why on earth did you do that?" Penny asked, her dark eyes wide with surprise.

"That's exactly what *they* asked," Jane said with a laugh. "But I decided that if I just went on taking the allowance, and I always knew I had it to fall back on, it would make having a job seem like showing off."

"Sort of like, 'see the rich girl work'?" Dee asked.

Jane nodded. "And I don't want it to be that way. So once I get a job, I'm in the same boat you are."

"Then welcome to the club." Dee leaned back on Andy's bed and smiled. "Sorry, Jane. Sometimes I have a big mouth."

"I think I've told you that before," teased Maggie, who had lots of experience smoothing hurt feelings caused by her blunt roommate.

Andy, who had been doing sit-ups on the floor, leaped to her feet and laughed. "Well, now that that's all settled, where are we going to eat?"

"Pizza Pete's, of course," Jane said with a grin. "I don't think one pizza with the works is too extravagant. Besides, the minute Dee mentioned it, my mouth started to water. If we don't eat pizza, my stomach will never forgive me."

"I've got an idea," Andy said, as she pulled on a pair of brightly flowered cotton shorts, "if Jane and I don't find jobs right away, we can borrow from Toby. She's been walking those dogs all day — she's probably ready to open a savings account."

At that moment, Toby walked in the door. Without a word, she strode to her bed, eased off her boots, and flopped down on her back, staring at the tea bag hanging from the ceiling.

The others looked at her, then at each other, and then back at Toby. Finally, Penny broke the silence. "You know, Toby," she said, "you remind me of a dream I had. I was on an up escalator in a department store, and the escalator stopped. And when I looked behind me, right down there at the bottom was a bear."

"A bear?" Maggie asked.

"A big brown bear." Penny's eyes sparkled — she loved to tell stories. "It was just getting ready to get on, and it was looking straight at me, so naturally I started running."

"Naturally," Dee commented.

"When I got to the top, I headed straight for the down escalator, and the bear followed," Penny went on. "This was a dream, remember, so for some reason, I didn't have the sense to leave the store. I just stayed on those broken escalators, running up and down, up and down. And that bear just kept on following me until I woke up."

Jane looked confused. "What does that have to do with Toby?"

"Well, can't you imagine? I was completely exhausted!" Penny burst out laughing. "I felt exactly the way Toby looks!"

Everyone turned back to Toby, who finally raised her head and spoke. "She's right, I'm completely tuckered out. Only it wasn't a bear, it was a dog. And it wasn't chasing me. I was chasing it."

Slowly sitting up, Toby told them about the dogs and what had happened after Charlie made his mad break for freedom. Randy jumped into his pickup truck, while Toby gathered the rest of the dogs and set off in the direction Charlie had gone. The dogs thought it was great fun, and ran so fast they almost pulled Toby off her feet. This time, though, she didn't care. All she wanted was to get Charlie before he skipped town.

Desperately trying to keep Randy's pickup in sight, Toby raced down the main street of Greenleaf, into a quiet neighborhood, through a few more hedges, across people's lawns and gardens, and finally came out on the same street where Mrs. Walters lived. Parked on the side was Randy's pickup.

"Did you lose him?" Toby called, running up to the truck.

Randy nodded. "Sorry. He cut through a yard and there was no way I could follow him."

Toby's heart sank. Charlie was gone, and she didn't have any choice but to tell Mrs. Walters. She couldn't keep on looking. Charlie could be anywhere by now, and besides, the rest of the dogs were tired. They'd flopped at her feet, panting and letting their tongues hang out.

Deciding she'd better face the music, Toby pulled the dogs to their feet and trudged down the street to Mrs. Walters' house. And there, on the porch, was Charlie.

"He was sitting there like he'd been waiting," Toby told the others now, "and he was smiling!" She sounded insulted. "That dog had played a joke on me and he was having the biggest laugh of his life."

"But he was back, right?" Andy said. "And

Mrs. Walters didn't even know what happened?"

"Wrong," Toby said. "Half the neighborhood had called her when they saw that mutt crashing through their flowers and bushes."

"Was she furious?" Maggie asked.

"I think she was so glad her 'baby' was okay that she forgot to be mad," Toby said. "But she didn't forget to fire me."

Andy's mouth dropped open. "She fired you?!"

"It wasn't even your fault!" Jane cried indignantly.

"Maybe it was," Toby said. "I knew Charlie had it in for me the minute he set eyes on me. I should have guessed he'd pull some kind of trick." She shook her head and couldn't help laughing. "Anyway, I spent the rest of the afternoon asking people if they needed their yards mowed and getting turned down. I had a job and lost it, all in one day. Must be some kind of record."

Jane was still offended. "I hope she at least had the decency to pay you."

"Oh, she paid me, all right." Toby pulled some crumpled bills from her jeans' pocket. "This is one day's wage, and believe me, I earned it."

"Well, great!" Andy said. "That's more than Jane and I earned today. We didn't get any work at all. But we're going to, right, Jane?"

"Right." Jane stood up and grabbed her purse. "Now let's pretend this day didn't even happen and go get some pizza!"

It was easy to pretend the day didn't exist while the six friends were enjoying one of Pizza Pete's finest creations. But later, after they'd come back to Baker House and gone to their rooms, Jane couldn't stop thinking about what had happened.

In the first place, the dorm was so quiet, Jane found it impossible to get to sleep. She never thought she'd miss the sounds of other girls' radios, and ringing telephones, and chatter. When she'd first come to Canby Hall, the noises had kept her awake. Now the silence was doing the same thing.

"Andy?" Jane waited, but there was no answer. "Toby?" No answer there, either. Both her roommates were asleep. Everybody's probably asleep, she thought. The campus clock had chimed twice just a few minutes before. Merry had looked in earlier, checking to see that everything was all right, and said she was turning in early. Dee and Maggie had to get up at an unbelievable hour, and they'd yawned most of the evening. Penny might be awake, Jane thought. She usually sat up late, working on the stories she loved to write. But Penny didn't have the same thing on her mind that Jane did — a job and how to get one.

As quietly as possible, Jane got out of bed and felt her way to her desk. The distance was all of about three feet, but she never knew what might be lurking there on the floor. This time, it was just a pair of shoes and her purse, so she made it without crashing and waking Andy. She wasn't worried about Toby, who slept like a log, but one of Andy's pet peeves was being waked up in the middle of the night.

Carefully, Jane felt along the top of her desk until her fingers touched the newspaper. With a quick flip, she tossed it onto her bed. So far, so good. Now for her keychain with the little penlight on it. She knew it was there; she'd tossed it on the desk when she came in. Stretching her hand out, she felt along the desktop. Suddenly her fingertips collided with something cool and metallic. Before she had time to react, one empty soda can toppled into another, and they both fell to the floor with a clang, rolling slowly and noisily until they clattered against the opposite wall.

"I heard that," Andy's voice said. "I heard it, and I didn't like it."

"Sorry," Jane whispered. She finally located the keychain and crept stealthily back onto her bed. Naturally, the springs creaked.

"I heard that, too," Andy announced immediately.

Jane suddenly decided the situation was ridiculous. "Well, as long as you're awake," she said with a giggle, "listen to this!" Feeling around for the newspaper, she began to turn the pages slowly and carefully, which only made the rustling and crackling seem louder.

"Okay, okay," Andy said, laughing softly. "You can stop trying to be quiet. It just makes it worse, like somebody taking forever to open a piece of candy at the movies."

"Good." Jane slid off her bed and snapped on her desk lamp. "There," she said. "Toby could sleep under a floodlight, and now that you're awake, I don't have to ruin my eyes reading with that tiny penlight."

Andy sat up, shading her eyes and squinting at Jane. "I know you want to find a job, but do you really think this is the time to do it?"

"No, but I couldn't sleep," Jane explained, bending over the Help Wanted ads, "and since this was on my mind, I thought I'd just take another look. I never finished reading them this afternoon, anyway."

"Well, let me know if something turns up." Andy said. "But let me know in the morning." Turning onto her stomach, she pulled the pillow over her head and burrowed around until she got comfortable.

Jane was already reading the ads, hoping to come across something new and exciting and perfect. Like the day before, there were plenty of jobs if you happened to be a secretary or a bookkeeper or a computer programmer. The ad for a dog walker was still there, she noticed with a wry smile. And there were a few new ones — some company wanted a bricklayer for an eight-week job, and someone else wanted their lawn mowed once a week.

Jane was just about to circle the lawn-mowing ad — after all, it was better than nothing — when she noticed another new one. " 'Family traveling in Europe needs reliable firm to prepare Greenleaf house for home-coming — $3\frac{1}{2}$ wks. Clean-up inside & out, some painting, repair work, and decorating. For details, write John Higgins, P.O. Box 721, Greenleaf.' "

Jane read the ad three times, and each time, it sounded better and better. The timing was perfect, because three and a half weeks was exactly how long she and Andy and Toby had left. By the time they got the job, it would probably be down to three weeks, but unless the house was a disaster, Jane knew they could do it. All three of them had painted rooms be-fore, and when it came to decorating, she was confident that her taste was as good as any-one's. And how hard was a clean-up? Mowing and watering the lawn, dusting and vacuum-ing the rooms? That would only take one day a week, with the three of them working at it.

"Andy?" Jane whispered excitedly. "Andy? Are you still awake?"

Andy's steady, even breathing didn't change.

"Andy!" Jane's voice rose slightly above a

whisper. "Wake up! I think I've found something!"

Andy mumbled something, rolled onto her back, and kept on sleeping.

"All right," Jane said. "I'll wait until morning." Circling the ad with a yellow felt-tipped marker, Jane turned off the lamp and stretched out in bed. How long would it take, she wondered? Two days? Three? Turning on her side, she smiled into the darkness. In two or three days, the firm of "Barrett, Cord, and Houston" just might have landed its first job.

CHAPTER
FIVE

Barrett, Cord, and Houston?" Toby stopped buttering her toast and gave Jane a skeptical look. "Sounds like a bunch of stuffy people in a stuffy office. Lawyers or something."

"I think it sounds very tasteful," Jane argued, stirring her coffee. "And it'll make people think we've been in business for years."

It was ten-thirty the next morning, and the three roommates were in a booth at The Greaf having breakfast. Or rather, Toby and Andy were having breakfast. Jane was so excited about the ad she'd found that she hadn't stopped talking about it long enough to eat.

"We have to write a letter to this John Higgins," Jane went on, "and we can't sign it 'Toby, Andy, and Jane.' It doesn't have the right ring to it. Besides, the ad said they were looking for a reliable firm."

Andy waved her fork in the air and quickly swallowed a bite of French toast. "Slow down a minute," she said. "What's the point of arguing about what to call ourselves when we haven't even decided to try for the job?"

"You're right," Toby laughed. "First things first."

Jane stared at them in amazement. "What do you mean, we haven't decided to try for the job?" she asked.

"Well, after all, we're not talking about fixing up a dormitory room or hammering together a rickety booth for the school carnival," Andy said. "We're talking about taking care of a whole house."

"It does seem like a pretty big bite," Toby agreed. "How do we know we won't choke on it?"

Still amazed, Jane set her blueberry muffin back on its plate. "Is this really Andrea Cord and October Houston talking to me?" she asked in disbelief. "The street-smart city girl and the fearless rider of the rattlesnake-infested plains? Afraid of a job like this?" Shaking her head, she picked up the muffin again and sliced it in half. "I'm shocked. I really am."

"Okay, okay, we get the point," Andy said with a laugh. "But, Jane, we have to be realistic. I mean, the ad says 'some repair work.' What does 'some' mean? What if they want us to do things with gutters and roofs and plaster? We don't know anything about stuff like that."

"Well, of course, if it's too much, we can't take it on," Jane admitted. "But we could at least find out. Maybe it's just one hole in the wall. How hard could something like that be? Besides," she added, spreading the muffin generously with strawberry jam, "Cary knows a lot about repair work, and I'm sure he'd be willing to give us some pointers."

Cary, who hadn't been consulted yet, was busy at the counter with five customers. Andy glanced at him and then back at Jane. "Cary's great," she said, "but he's just one guy. I keep telling you, Jane, this is a big job."

"We'll never know how big until we ask." Jane's muffin, still uneaten, was put on its plate again. "I just can't believe you don't want to ask."

"It's not that I don't want to," Andy told her. "I guess you were right — I guess I am a little scared."

"Of what?"

"I'll tell you what *I'm* scared of," Toby said. "With any other job, there'd be somebody watching over us all the time, to make sure we do it right. But with this one, we'd be on our own."

"But that's what we want, isn't it?" Jane cried. "That's why we decided to stay — to work and be on our own."

For a few minutes, no one said anything. While Toby and Andy thought about the job, Jane finally ate her muffin and waited for them to agree with her. She was almost positive they would. She'd practically called them cowards, and if nothing else would make them see things her way, she knew that would, because they weren't cowards. Besides, nobody had a job right now. If they didn't go after this one, they'd be right back where they started.

"Well," Andy said finally, "I guess it won't hurt to check it out."

Toby nodded. "We'd be nuts not to. And if it turns out to be a real colossal job, and we can't handle it, we'll just keep looking."

"We can handle it," Jane said confidently. "I know we can. What's a little lawn-mowing and painting? And when it comes to decorating, I can take care of that part."

"Hey, what about me?" Andy asked, pretending to be insulted. "You're not the only one with good taste, you know."

Toby laughed. Both of them had good taste; it was just that they were complete opposites. Jane liked the traditional, and Andy went in for modern things. "Don't be so sure *I* won't have anything to say about this decorating business," she teased. "For all you know, these people might love the western look. And I'm the expert on rawhide and horse blankets."

"And tea bags," Andy added. Toby had never told anyone the meaning of the tea bag that hung over her bed, and Andy thought now might be a good chance to find out. "I suppose no authentic western home would be without at least one tea bag dangling from the ceiling, right?"

Toby laughed again and shook her head, but she didn't have to answer. At that moment, Cary arrived at their table. "A break at last," he sighed, sinking into the booth beside Jane. "Just a few more hours and I can go jump in the swimming pool. Hey, why don't we all go?"

"Sounds great!" Andy said.

"Yep," Toby agreed. "A nice, cool dip in the water sounds just about perfect."

"If there's time," Jane reminded them. "Don't forget, we've got a very important letter to write." Turning to Cary, she told him about the ad she'd found and how the three of them had decided to apply for the job.

Cary gave a low whistle. "Well, good luck if you get it," he said skeptically.

After almost convincing Toby and Andy that they *could* do it, Jane wasn't in the mood to argue with Cary. Besides, she thought that he, of all people, would be the one to tell her to go for it. "You sound like you think we're completely incompetent," she said coolly.

Cary shook his head. "That's not true," he told her. "But it's a big job. I'm just being realistic."

Jane's chin went up. "Thanks. But one

of the things you've always accused me of is being *too* realistic. Not having any sense of adventure."

"She's got you there, Cary," Andy pointed out.

Cary laughed and threw up his hands. "Okay, okay!" he said. "But if you see the place and it turns out to be too much, don't be afraid to turn it down."

"We won't," Jane assured him. "But I just know it's not going to be too much. I have a feeling it's going to be the perfect summer job. Now all we have to do is come up with the right name for our letter. I like 'Barrett, Cord, and Houston,' but Toby thinks that's too stuffy. What about you?"

Cary tilted his head back and closed his eyes. When he opened them, they were sparkling. He'd obviously had a brainstorm. "I've got it," he said, "and it's a beauty. How about, '407, Inc.'?"

Later that day, after a refreshing swim in the local pool and a picnic of cheese, crackers, and fruit by Canby Hall's wishing pond, the members of "407, Inc." sat down to compose their letter to John Higgins. Meredith had one of the fanciest electric typewriters in the dorm, and after hearing the story, she had agreed to let the three roommates use it. Meredith's quarters on the fifth floor of Baker House had sloping ceilings, a thick beige carpet, lots of green plants, and a lived-in look that made the girls feel welcome.

"I just hope you know what you might be getting into," Meredith said as Andy sat down at her desk to get used to the typewriter. "I don't want to sound preachy, but this job would be a big responsibility."

"Not you, too!" Jane wailed. "Everyone I've talked to has tried to warn me away from this job! I thought part of Canby Hall's philosophy was to promote independence."

Merry couldn't help laughing. "I see you've been listening to Ms. Allardyce," she said. "And she's right — Canby Hall does want its students to be independent and responsible."

"Well?" Jane asked. "What could be more independent and responsible than taking on this job?"

Merry leaned back in one of her overstuffed easy chairs and thought a minute. When she'd first come to Canby Hall, none of the girls had trusted her. She'd been so scared of being too easy on them that she'd gone too far in the other direction and clamped down like a vise, enforcing every rule like a police officer and passing out demerit slips like candy. Things were fine now, but still, she couldn't be just another pal to the girls. She was older, she was the grown-up, and besides, she had her responsibilities, too.

"I guess what I'm trying to say is, be sure you're ready for the job before you take it."

"If we get it," Toby pointed out.

"Which we never will if we don't write this letter," Andy reminded them. "Come on, I've got the date and the address typed in. What do we say next?"

Meredith decided that once was enough to give her opinion and joined in as they all tried to figure out what to say and how to say it. After a lot of joking around and two breaks for lemonade, they finally came up with something they all agreed was short but impressive. Without lying — in fact, they knew they had to admit that they were students — they told John Higgins that they were completely capable of doing the job he needed done, but that since they were inexperienced, they'd do it for less money that he'd have to pay an established company. That had been Meredith's idea.

"I don't know what jobs like this pay," she said, "but I'm sure it's more than you'd earn waiting tables or shelving library books, so there's no reason to be greedy. If he's worried about your experience, maybe the thought of saving money will change his mind."

"Right," Andy agreed. "And no matter what we make, it'll be more than we're making right now."

When the letter was finished, Jane put in a couple of photographs — one of her bedroom in Boston and the other of the dining room, both of which she'd helped decorate. Then the three roommates hurried downstairs to get to the mailbox in time for the last pickup of the day.

"There is goes," Toby said as Jane dropped it in. "I guess all we can do now is wait."

"And keep our fingers crossed," Andy added. "I know I wasn't very excited about this job at first, but writing that letter convinced me we can do it."

"Of course we can." Jane had never doubted it, but now that it was out of their hands, she felt frustrated. Toby was right — all they could do was wait.

No one expected to hear anything the day after they'd sent the letter, but just in case, Jane thought that someone ought to be in the room from nine to five to answer the telephone. Andy volunteered to take the morning, Toby relieved her at about noon, and Jane came back from the swimming pool at two-thirty.

"Anything?" she asked as she walked into the room.

Toby shook her head. "I was beginning to think that phone forgot how to ring," she said. "I had Penny call me just to make sure it was working."

Jane looked worried. "I hope Mr. Higgins didn't pick that exact minute to call."

"If he did, he'll call back," Toby said, calmly pulling on her boots so she could go riding at the Crowell farm.

But Jane couldn't be calm about it. She'd been tempted to start biting her nails the minute they'd mailed that letter, and she knew she wouldn't relax until they heard something.

After Toby left, Jane stretched out on her bed, her hair still damp and smelling of chlorine. But she didn't dare take a shower until after five o'clock. Andy was still at the pool, and there was no one else to get the phone.

At ten minutes of five, it finally rang. Not wanting to seem too eager and desperate, Jane forced herself to wait until after the second ring to pick it up.

"407," she said, in what she hoped was an efficient, businesslike tone of voice.

"Hi!" Cary said. "I just had a great idea. They're playing music in Bradbury Park tonight. Why don't we grab some pizza and then go see what kind of sound the Greenleaf Music Ensemble can come up with?"

Jane's shoulders slumped and she sighed. "That'll be fun, I guess."

"Hey, don't get too excited, now," Cary joked. "I'm not promising the most fantastic night of your life."

"I'm sorry," Jane told him. "I was just hoping it was somebody else."

"Oh?" Cary's voice was slightly less teasing. "Well, I do like honesty, that's for sure."

"I didn't mean that the way it sounded," Jane said, smiling into the phone. "I was hoping it was John Higgins — you know, about the house."

"Come on, Jane," Cary said. "Sitting around waiting for the phone to ring is a waste of time."

"Well, it is now," Jane said, glancing at her watch. "It's after business hours."

"Right, so let's go have some fun," Cary urged. "I'd try to talk you into going even if it weren't after business hours," he chuckled. "You know what they say about watched pots."

"Well, of course I'm coming with you," Jane replied. "But that saying about watched pots isn't true. They do boil."

The pot boiled the next morning. And nobody was watching. At nine-twenty, all three roommates were still asleep, even Toby, who'd sat up late the night before comparing Texas and Georgia with Penny. Andy had practiced some dance steps at the auditorium until she was satisfied she'd got them right, and then joined Dee and Maggie and Meredith for a movie on Meredith's VCR. Much to Jane's disappointment, the Greenleaf Music Ensemble played only two classical pieces, while the rest were what Cary called "advanced elevator music." But it had been fun, anyway.

And the next morning, as usual, Jane punched the snooze button on her alarm until it gave up trying to do its job.

When the phone rang, Toby didn't budge, while Jane groaned and turned onto her back. Andy, who waked at the drop of a sock, cleared her throat a few times, and then picked up the receiver.

"407," she said, remembering that this was supposed to be a place of business.

"John Higgins here," a friendly voice answered. "I got your letter, and I think we should talk."

Frantically, Andy reached around for something to toss at Jane. Her hand closed over one of her stuffed animals — a dilapidated cat named Moe — and she pitched it right at Jane's head. "Yes," she said into the phone, "we'd be very interested in talking, Mr. Higgins."

Jane was stirring now, trying to push the hairy creature away from her face. At the name "Higgins," her eyes flew open, and she sat straight up in bed like a puppet being pulled on a string.

"Is it him?" she mouthed to Andy.

Andy nodded and gave her a thumbs-up sign. "Yes, Mr. Higgins. Ten-thirty is fine." Stretching to her desk, she grabbed a pad and pencil and wrote down the address. "Yes, I've got it," she said. "Who? Oh, Ms. Jane Barrett. She's in charge of all of 407's job contracts.

She's the one to talk to. Thank you, Mr. Higgins. Good-bye."

Hanging up the phone, Andy reached for another stuffed animal — a floppy dog with a big pink bow around its neck — and tossed it triumphantly into the air. "We passed the first test!" she cried.

Jane was laughing with excitement, hopping up and down on her bed, and both of them were making enough noise to finally rouse Toby.

"What's going on?" Toby asked, peering at them with sleepy eyes.

"An interview for a job!" Andy told her. "With Mr. John Higgins. I don't believe it!"

Toby rubbed her eyes and grinned. "I didn't think we had a chance in a million."

"Didn't I tell you?" Jane said. "I just knew it was going to happen. And you'll see, by eleven o'clock this morning, '407, Inc.' is going to be in business!"

CHAPTER SIX

Getting ready for such an important meeting was not something Jane usually did in a hurry. In fact, getting ready for anything in the morning took a lot of thought and care, mainly because she was almost always half asleep until eleven, at least.

But this morning, there was no time to snooze and stretch, take a long wake-up shower, and then try on different outfits until she found the right one.

Fortunately, Jane was willing to sacrifice leisure time for the sake of the job. Also fortunately, she had Toby and Andy to help her. While she took a record-breaking, three-minute shower, Toby went through her closet and pulled out her clothes for her. And the minute Jane came back, Andy was there with the blow-dryer, aiming it at her head the entire time Jane got dressed.

"We make a great team," Jane said grate-

fully, brushing her nearly-dry hair. "Should
I wear makeup?"

Andy put her head on one side and looked
at her. "A touch," she announced. "Just the
tiniest bit of eye shadow. We don't want Mr.
Higgins to think you're a complete babe in
the woods."

"He won't," Toby said. "Look at her — she
looks like she does this every day of her life."

Her hair in place, wearing low-heeled shoes
and a light brown cotton dress that had been
made by her mother's dressmaker, Jane did
look poised and confident. Inside, the butter-
flies were starting to swoop around her
stomach, but nobody, including John Higgins,
would ever have guessed.

At twenty minutes after ten, Jane turned
and waved to Andy and Toby as they went
into The Greaf to wait for her. Then she
walked two more blocks until she found the
address John Higgins had given to Andy. It
was a small house divided into the offices of a
real estate company and a lawyer. John Higgins was the lawyer. Straightening her
shoulders, Jane took a deep breath and
stepped inside.

"I can't eat," Andy announced ten minutes
later. "This is almost as bad as waiting to get
a term paper back." She pushed her half-
nibbled muffin aside and took a sip of milk.
"What happens if he decides not to hire us?

I mean, I haven't even been checking the want ads since we mailed that letter."

Toby, who could probably have eaten even during a hurricane, finished the last bite of her scrambled eggs. "I've been checking them," she said calmly.

Andy stared at her. "You have? Did you tell Jane?"

"Now why would I do that?" Toby asked. "She'd think I was going behind her back or something, and she'd get mad. All I was doing was trying to find something to fall back on, in case this didn't work out. Made sense to me."

"Me, too," Andy agreed. "I should have done the same thing. Did you find anything?"

Toby shrugged. "There's still not much to pick from, but I spotted a couple of lawn-mowing and baby-sitting jobs. I was going to check them out today if Mr. Higgins didn't call."

"Well, don't throw out that paper," Andy warned. "We still might need it." The thought that there might possibly be other jobs brought back Andy's appetite, and she waved Cary over.

"A muffin's not enough," she said, when he arrived. "I'd like a side order of bacon, too."

"Coming right up." Cary wrote down the order and then leaned against their table. "Do you think I should tell the cook to get something ready for Jane?" he asked. "You said she had to miss breakfast and I know what that means — she'll be so weak from hunger she'll probably have to drag herself in here."

Andy laughed. "I think you'd better wait. If it's good news, she'll probably want twice what she usually eats. And if it's bad news, she'll be too depressed for anything but coffee."

After Cary went into the kitchen, Randy Crowell walked through the door of the diner. Spotting Toby and Andy, he strolled over and joined them. "My truck's getting a once-over," he said, "so I thought I'd grab a snack in here. How's the job-hunting going?"

When Toby explained the situation, Randy decided to stay until Jane arrived. "It'll take a while for my truck to be ready, and besides, if you get the job, that'll call for a celebration. Hey!" he went on, "how about everybody coming out to the farm for a ride this afternoon? Even if you don't get the job?"

"I'm ready for that," Toby said quickly. "If I don't get on a horse at least twice a week, I'm afraid I might turn into a city-slicker."

"Speaking of city-slickers," Andy reminded them, "I'm one. I'm used to riding a bus, not a horse."

Toby grinned. "Well, horses are mighty tricky sometimes," she said. "They can smell a city-slicker a mile away, and when one of them gets on their backs, they like to show 'em who's boss."

Randy laughed. "Don't worry, Andy, I've got the perfect horse for you. He's a real gentleman — if he wants to get rid of a rider, he just sits down and slides them off."

Andy was still getting teased about her horseback riding ability when Cary came back with the plate of bacon. As he set it down, he glanced toward the front windows and saw a familiar blonde-haired girl heading for the door. "Okay, everybody, keep your fingers crossed," he said excitedly. "Jane's on her way in."

Although the four at the table could usually tell what kind of mood Jane was in just by looking at her face and watching the way she walked, this time she didn't give them a clue. Moving at a steady pace, her face expressionless, Jane made her way across the diner.

"Well?" Andy asked impatiently. "Don't keep us in suspense. What happened?"

For an answer, Jane reached into her bag and took something out. Then, her face finally breaking into a big smile, she dangled a set of keys from her finger.

"We got it?" Toby and Andy asked together.

"We got it!" Jane announced, dropping the keys on the table. "I want the biggest breakfast on The Greaf's menu!"

Everyone laughed and congratulated her, and while Cary went off to place the order for the "Paul Bunyan Special," Jane described what had happened.

"It couldn't have been better," she said. "Mr. Higgins is Ms. Browen's cousin. Browen," she added, "that's the owner's name. Mr. Higgins has been trying to get somebody to do this job for weeks. But all the regular companies he's talked to are filled up. So he said our letter came at just the right time. I didn't have to say much of anything," she laughed. "He was ready to hire us the minute I walked through the door."

"What did he say about the job?" Andy asked. "Exactly what do we have to do?"

"Pretty much what the ad said," Jane told her. "Cleaning inside and out. Shampooing the rugs. Painting the living room."

"What about the repair job?" Toby asked.

"It's some steps that lead up to an outside deck," Jane said. "All we have to do is hammer new ones on. And the decorating part's really going to be fun. It's a sun porch. Some paint, some plants, and some summery furniture, and it'll be beautiful."

Cary came back then, and with a flourish, set a platter piled with buckwheat cakes, bacon, and eggs in front of her. Jane started to dig in and then stopped. "I almost forgot the very best part," she said. Reaching into her bag again, she pulled out what was obviously a check. "This is half of what we're going to earn. We'll get the second half when we finish."

Cary and Randy both gave out low whistles, and Toby and Andy stared at the check as if it were made out of gold.

"One thousand five hundred dollars?" Andy's voice almost squeaked. "You mean he's going to pay us three thousand dollars?!"

Toby finally found her voice. "I'll be," she said, and then clammed up again.

"This isn't all for us, of course," Jane explained. "We'll have to buy the paint and things, and rent a carpet cleaner, and buy a couple of pieces of furniture for the sun porch. But if we're careful, there should be plenty left over to divide up."

"I think I'm in the wrong business," Cary quipped.

"Me, too." Randy laughed. "Looks like you three landed a great job."

Jane ate a few bites of food. Then she set her fork down. "I'm too excited to eat. Let's go out to the house and plan what to do first."

"Good idea," Andy said. "I can't wait to see it."

Cary was able to get a break then and Randy discovered that the mechanics had done all they could for his pickup, so the five of them piled in and headed to the Browens' house.

The drive took them into a section of

Greenleaf not too far from the campus, where large, expensive houses had been built, and where huge oak and maple trees towered over well-kept flower gardens.

"Number sixteen, there it is!" Jane called out, and Randy turned the pickup into a short, winding drive lined with trees and littered with leaves and branches blown down during the winter. As he pulled to a stop in front of the white house, they all stared at it for a moment.

"It's a big one, isn't it?" Toby commented.

"It sure is," Andy said. "I'm glad we don't have to paint the outside."

"It could use a new coat," Randy remarked, climbing out of the truck.

"Well, that's not part of the deal, so let's not worry about it," Jane said, walking toward the front door. "Come on, let's go inside."

The front door opened into a large entrance hall, about three times the size of Room 407. At the back was an oak staircase leading to the second floor, and on either side, curved and molded doorways led into the living and dining rooms. It was a beautiful house, but it was hot and musty-smelling, and Toby wrinkled her nose.

"Let's start work right now by getting some air in here," she suggested. Striding to a window in the living room, she reached for the lever that cranked open the two outside panes of stained glass.

"Wait!" Jane called out. "I almost forgot, all the windows are wired."

Toby immediately dropped her hand. "Wired with *what?*"

"It's an alarm system," Jane explained. Taking several sheets of paper from her purse, she scanned them until she found the right one. "Here. Yes, the switch to turn off the alarm is in the kitchen," she said. "I'll go do that and then we can air all the rooms."

After Jane had left, the others looked at the living room. Or rather, the walls of the living room, which were covered in a dark, forest-green paint.

"I can see why they want it white," Andy commented. "This room's like a dungeon with green walls."

"Better buy plenty of paint," Randy remarked. "It'll take more than one coat to cover that green."

"There," Jane said, coming back in. "The alarm's off. It was right where he said it would be."

"You mean this is the first time you've seen the house?" Andy asked.

"Yes," Jane said. "Mr. Higgins was leaving town at noon and he didn't have time to show it to me." Cranking open some windows, which had screens on the inside, she added, "But he gave me a complete list of everything, and he'll be back in about two weeks, so that's no problem."

"No, I mean, I thought you must have looked at the house before you accepted the job," Andy told her. "Just to see what we'd have to do."

"Why should I do that?" Jane asked. "He told me *exactly* what we'd have to do." Opening the French doors on one wall of the living room, she walked into the sun porch.

Cary raised his eyebrows and followed her, but Andy stayed behind, shaking her head. "Do you see the size of this thing?" she asked, pointing to a beautiful, but very big, Oriental rug. "If it weren't so pretty, we could play football on it."

"There's another one just like it in the dining room," Toby said. "And I'll bet the bedrooms aren't bare planks. Looks like we'll keep the rug shampoo company in business for a while."

"The outside isn't going to be a piece of cake, either," Randy pointed out. "They've got a big hunk of land here, and right now it's a mess. It doesn't look like it's been touched since the end of last summer."

"Come on," Toby suggested. "Let's go check it out."

As the three of them went outside, Cary, who had been standing in the doorway of the sun porch, put his hand on Jane's shoulder. "Did Mr. Higgins leave a number where you can reach him?" he asked.

"Oh, yes, of course," Jane said, her eyes

wandering over cartons and boxes and rickety pieces of furniture. The sun porch had obviously been used for storage. "He said to call him if we have any questions at all. Why?"

Cary cleared his throat. He wasn't sure how to say it, and he didn't want to get Jane angry, but he honestly thought this job was going to be too much. "Oh, I was just checking. I mean, now that you've seen the place, are you still sure you want to do it?"

Jane knew exactly what he meant. And she understood why he was saying it. After all, she wasn't blind; she'd seen the color of the living room and the size of the rugs as well as anybody. Plus, there was all the furniture to be polished, and windows to be washed, not to mention what had to be done outside.

It was going to be hard, Jane had to admit that. But she wasn't about to admit that it might be too hard. "Of course I still want to do it," she said to Cary. "It's going to take a lot of planning and organization, and like Andy says, I'm not a great organizer. But I can be when I want to, and I want to now. Besides, it's going to be fun." Smiling, she put her arm around his waist. "You'll see, we're all going to have a great time."

CHAPTER SEVEN

In spite of their doubts, Andy and Toby got up the next morning as eager to go to work as Jane. "After all," Andy had said to Toby the night before, "we can't quit before we start." They realized that they were all in it together, and besides, getting a job was the reason they'd decided to stay on at Canby Hall. If they didn't take this one, another one might not come along until it was too late.

Instead of eating breakfast at the diner, the roommates bought fruit, muffins, and cartons of milk and orange juice and biked to the house. They ate while they discussed their "plan of attack," as Andy called it.

Wearing jeans, tennis shoes, and bright, oversized T-shirts, they let themselves onto the deck through the upstairs master bedroom, wiped the winter's accumulation of dirt and leaves from the redwood table and benches and sat down to eat.

"We should leave the easy things for last," Jane said, reaching for an apple-cinnamon muffin. "We can take down the curtains today or tomorrow, wash the ones that can be washed, and send the others to the dry cleaners. But we won't put them back up until practically the last day."

Andy had to laugh. "I never thought I'd hear Jane Barrett talking about washing curtains," she quipped.

Jane smiled dryly. "I'm not quite as ignorant as I used to be," she said. "Thanks to doing my own laundry at Canby Hall, I now know the difference between bleach and fabric softener."

Toby reached for an orange and grinned. "Isn't education wonderful?"

"All right, you two." Jane laughed and took another bite of muffin. "I may not be an expert, but I'm making sense, aren't I?"

Andy nodded. "Sure. Why put the curtains back up before we dust and polish? And why dust and polish right now? Then we'd wind up having to do it again. If we wait, we'll only have to do it once, right before the Browens' come home."

"Good," Toby said. "I'm not too fond of dusting and polishing, anyway."

"Of course, we can't leave the rugs until the very end," Jane went on. "We can do those somewhere in the middle. The same for the steps."

Toby chewed an orange section and thought a minute. "That leaves painting, decorating, and cleaning the yard," she said. "Where do we start?"

After another half hour of discussion, the members of "407, Inc." decided to start on the yard. The garage was well-equipped with rakes, shovels, hoses, and a lawn mower; the roommates were full of breakfast and energy, and the sun was bright in a cloudless sky. Outdoors was the perfect place to be.

It was ten-thirty when they began. An hour later, Jane dumped what felt like a ton of twigs and tree limbs into an ever-growing pile at the end of the drive. As she started to walk back into the yard, the honk of a car horn made her stop and turn.

Patrice Allardyce, Canby Hall's headmistress, leaned her head out of a smart-looking, silver-gray sedan and frowned with confusion as Jane walked over to her. "I thought that was you, Jane," she said. "What on earth are you doing at the Browens' house?"

Jane pushed her damp hair back from her face and smiled. "Oh, do you know them, Ms. Allardyce?"

"Quite well," the headmistress said. "They're lovely people. I was certain they were still out of town, though."

"They are," Jane told her. "Toby and Andy and I have to have the house ready for them by the time they get back. It's our job."

"You mean they hired you?"

"Not exactly," Jane said. "Their cousin did. He put an ad in the paper, we answered it, and he hired us. Today's our first day."

Ms. Allardyce's eyebrows rose slightly in surprise. "I'm familiar with that house," she commented. "I must say, it's an awfully big job."

"Yes," Jane agreed. "But I'm sure we can do it." It seemed like she'd been saying that for two days straight. Why wouldn't anyone believe her?

"Hey, Jane!" Andy's voice called loudly. "What are you doing out here? Taking a nap?"

Andy and Toby, their arms full of more dead branches, emerged from around the end of the drive. When they saw P.A., as most Canby Hallers called the headmistress behind her back, they stopped, breathing hard.

"Jane was just telling me about your job," Ms. Allardyce said, eyeing their scratched arms and perspiring faces. "I know the Browens, and I'm quite impressed that you three would take on their house. I'm sure you'll do your best."

"Yes, ma'am," Toby said, wiping her forehead with the back of her hand. "We aim to do just that."

"Good. Well, I must be going." The headmistress started to put the car in gear, but then stopped. "I had planned to invite all the girls who've remained at Canby Hall to my house for tea sometime soon. Can I expect you to accept, or will you be too busy?"

"Oh, no," Jane assured her. Tea with Ms. Allardyce was an honor and turning down honors was something that just wasn't done. "We won't be too busy at all. We spent most of this morning planning our work schedule, and it leaves us with plenty of free time."

"Does it?" The headmistress's eyebrows rose again, but she didn't comment. "Well, then, I'll be sending the invitations out in the next few days, so I'm glad to hear you'll be able to accept. Oh, one more thing," she went on. "You can't leave that pile of branches there. The sanitation crew only picks them up twice a year — fall and spring. You'll have to arrange to get rid of them yourselves or you might be fined." With a nod and a smile, she drove off.

For a few minutes, the three roommates just stared at the branches they'd spent the last hour lugging to the end of the drive. Finally, Jane spoke. "It's simple," she said, trying to sound enthusiastic. "We just pull them back, out of sight, and no one will spot them. Then we can keep piling them here until we're ready to have them taken away." She wasn't sure who was going to take them away, but she decided to worry about that later. After all, there was plenty of time.

Pulling them out of sight took another half

hour, and by then, the sun was straight up in the sky, its rays beating down like a hot, steady rain.

"I can hear the freckles popping out on my face," Toby said.

"We should have worn hats," Andy said. "Blacks can get sunburned, too, you know."

Jane, whose face was flushed a bright shade of rose, tossed the last load of branches onto the new pile, and sat down next to it. "I'm starving," she announced. "Let's eat, buy some sunscreen, and sunhats, and then finish the job this afternoon."

Since the other two were as hot and worn-out as Jane, they weren't about to argue with her.

"A little food and we'll be back in shape in no time," Toby said, as they biked to town and the diner.

"A little food and about a gallon of ice water," Andy added.

"About a gallon apiece," Jane said. "My tongue feels big and sandy."

"Back home in Texas, we call that parched," Toby told her.

"Back home in Boston," Jane said, "we call it dehydrated."

"Back home in Chicago, we call it thirsty," Andy said, and they were all laughing when they walked into The Greaf.

It was the lunch hour, and the diner was crowded. The parched, dehydrated, and thirsty roommates stood in the entrance, hoping to spot an empty booth. No one wanted to sit at the counter; they needed something to lean back on.

From his station behind the counter, Cary saw them and walked over. Jane's hair was matted and tangled, one of Andy's shirt sleeves was torn, and part of a small branch had caught on the hem of Toby's jeans. All three had scratches on their arms, dust streaks on their faces, and leaves clinging to their clothes.

"Aha! You've been exploring nature, I see," Cary quipped.

"Very funny," Jane said, giving his arm a light backhand punch. "You know very well we've been working at our job. Now do yours and find us a booth."

"Otherwise," Andy warned, "we might just collapse right here and ruin everybody's appetite."

Deadpan, Toby added, "In fact, I'm beginnin' to feel a little green around the gills right this very minute."

"Okay, okay." Cary held up his hands in mock surrender. "I can tell you're not in the mood for jokes. So I'll get serious — we're filled up. But," he went on quickly, "three of your Baker House buddies are here, and if they don't object to your appearance, which, I might add, is almost against The Greaf's dress code, I'm sure they won't mind sharing their luncheon space."

His speech finished, Cary bowed from the waist and waved the three roommates toward a booth where Maggie, Dee, and Penny were sitting. The "Baker House buddies" shifted and readjusted their seating, and then Dee, as usual, came right to the point. "You guys look like you've been through the wringer. How are you going to make it through three more weeks?"

"I've been asking myself that same question all morning," Andy admitted. Then, as Jane shot her a stern look, she said, "But don't worry, we'll make it."

"You know," Penny said, "ya'll make me feel real lazy. Here I am, just spending my time sunnin' and swimmin', while the rest of you are working like dogs."

"Shameful," Toby said.

Andy crunched an ice cube and nodded. "Maybe you'd like to help us out."

Penny laughed. "I never thought of that, but why not? Tell you what, you find yourselves in a pickle, you be sure to call on me."

"How about us?" Maggie teased. "After all, Dee and I are working, too, wearing our fingers to the bone for the Dewey Decimal System."

"Yes, but you're working in an air-conditioned library," Penny pointed out. "These poor souls are breaking their backs under the broiling sun."

"Honestly, it's not as bad as that," Jane

said, picking up her second glass of water. "This is the just the worst part, that's all. After we finish the yard, it's going to be easy."

"At least it's not boring, like the library," Dee said. "Doing the same thing every day makes me feel like a robot. I have to swim for an hour afterward to get my brain working again."

"Don't mention swimming to me," Andy sighed. "It sounds so good, I might just go jump in the pool right now, clothes and all."

"I'd be right behind you," Toby said.

"Well, there's no reason we can't go swimming," Jane told them. "Did you think we were going to work from dawn to dusk?"

"I already feel like we did," Andy joked. "I always thought dance practice was hard, but after this morning, it's going to seem like playing."

"It's just because we're not used to it," Jane said. "Anyway, we're not going to work every day until we drop. We'll stop work when everybody else does." Turning to the other three, she said, "In fact, we'll meet you at the pool at about three o'clock."

As it turned out, only Jane went to the pool that afternoon. Quitting work at two-thirty, the roommates went back to Baker House for a shower, and while they were still in their room, peeling off their dirty clothes, the phone rang.

"407," Jane answered, just in case it was Mr. Higgins. "Oh, hello, Matt. Yes, she's right here."

Breaking into a big smile, Andy took the phone. "Hi! Are you in town?"

"No, but I will be next week," Matt's soft voice answered.

"Great!" As Jane and Toby went off to shower, Andy curled up on her bed and started to tell Matt all about their job. She was just hanging up when they got back. back.

"How's Matt?" Toby asked, rubbing her hair with a bright yellow towel, and wishing she had just spoken to Neal.

"Fine," Andy said. "He's coming to Greenleaf next week to spend the day with me. Isn't that great? I can't wait to see him." Reaching for her robe and towel, Andy went on, "He went to the ballet last night. Hearing him talk about it made my feet itch for a pair of ballet shoes. I haven't been practicing much, and I've got to keep in shape. I think I'll go over to the auditorium and work on some steps. I can always swim tomorrow."

As Andy left the room, Toby reached for a clean pair of jeans instead of her swimming suit. Noticing the questioning look on Jane's face, she explained, "I just got a hankering."

"Is that Texan for an urge?" Jane asked dryly.

"Yep." Toby sat down and started pulling on her boots. "Swimming's great, but there's nothing like a horseback ride to really relax a person."

"Not this person," Jane laughed. "All I want to do right now is jump in that nice, cool water."

Later, at the auditorium, Andy loosened up and then turned on the tape recorder she'd brought with her. As the music started, she lifted her arms, paused for a beat, and then began to dance. Leaping and whirling gracefully around the stage, she forgot that just a few hours before, she'd been complaining about how tired she was. Dancing was work, too, but it was different. For Andy, dancing was also pure pleasure.

While Andy was losing herself in the movement of dance, Toby was urging her horse into a gentle lope across the fields of the Crowell farm. Beside her rode Randy, who had felt like a ride himself.

"I could do this all day long," Toby called out to him.

Randy laughed. "Listen, you might not be able to ride *all* day while you're here, but you can sure ride *every* day if you want."

"Thanks," Toby said. "I think I'll take you up on that." Tapping the horse lightly with her heels, she urged her to move a little faster.

"Better get going!" she called over her
shoulder to Randy, "or I'll leave you in the
dust!"

While Randy and Toby were galloping toward a hillside, Jane was pulling herself out of
the pool, breathing hard from her swim, but
completely refreshed by it.

Slinging her wet hair back from her face,
Jane waved to Maggie, Dee, and Penny, who
were just leaving to change and go back to
Baker. Jane was trying to decide whether to
join them or to swim a while longer, when she
saw a slim, light-brown-haired boy wearing a
blue bathing suit and a small gold earring
walking toward her. It was Cary, and she immediately decided to stay.

"You look like a brand-new girl," Cary
said, joining her at the edge of the pool.

"I feel like one," Jane told him. "Of course,
I still wouldn't pass The Greaf's dress code."

"Come on, I was just kidding about that,"
Cary protested, letting his feet dangle in the
water.

"Oh, I know." Jane slipped into the pool
and hung onto the edge, facing Cary. Grinning, she scooped up a handful of water and
splashed it at him. "But you come from a
proper Boston family, too," she teasingly reminded him, "even though you don't like to
admit it. I'm sure you were brought up not

to comment on the way somebody looks, so I'm just paying you back." Laughing, she splashed him again.

"Jane, Jane, you always look good to me." Cary was laughing, too, trying to dodge the sprays of water. "Hey, I bet I could turn that into a song."

"Not another song with my name in it!" Jane said. When they'd first met, and Jane had refused to go out with him, Cary had stood under the window of 407, singing his own composition which started, "Jane, Jane, won't you come out and play?" "I don't think I could stand the embarrassment," she joked, this time drenching him with water.

"Now I'm insulted!" Still laughing, Cary pushed himself off the edge of the pool and landed in the water beside Jane. "I warn you, I've been the All-City Water-Fight Champion for the past three years." Slapping his hand against the water, he shot a spray directly at Jane's head.

"Well, get ready!" Jane told him. "You're about to lose your title!"

And as the two of them laughed and joked and splashed each other, Jane completely forgot about the scratches on her arms and the ache in her back. And it didn't matter that they'd only cleared half the yard of branches that day. The house would still be there tomorrow.

CHAPTER EIGHT

Toby's eyes usually popped open at the first hint of morning, and after a stretch and a yawn, she'd be wide awake and ready to start the day.

The morning after their first day at the Browens' house, Toby's eyes opened on schedule, but there was a difference — they didn't pop, they cracked. Not quite sure what was wrong, she sat up and rubbed them. The minute her hands touched her face, she knew what the problem was: she was sunburned, and from the way her skin felt, she was sunburned bad.

"You look like a lobster," Andy observed from her bed. "Your eyes are two slits in red paper. Does it hurt?"

"Only when I blink," Toby groaned. "I guess by the time I put that sunscreen on, it was too late."

"Looks like I got lucky," Andy said. But

when she pushed herself up, she groaned, too. "My arms! My arms feel like somebody stomped on them."

"Maybe you shouldn't have danced after all that work we did," Toby suggested, gingerly touching her face with her fingertips.

"I don't dance on my arms," Andy pointed out. "It wasn't the dancing, and it wasn't just the work, either. After all, I'm in good shape. It's just that I'm not used to carrying a ton of branches around."

"Maybe you'd *better* start dancing on your arms, then. Get them in shape, too." Toby grinned and then winced. "Ow! I can't smile, either."

As the two of them got up and stretched, a low moan came from Jane's bed. "I think I pulled a muscle in my back," a groggy voice said. "I don't think I can roll over." With another moan and a lot of struggling, Jane finally managed to get herself to the edge of the bed. Carefully, she eased herself to a sitting position and then stood up. "I guess it's not pulled," she said, rubbing her back. "But it certainly is sore."

The three of them stood in silence for a minute, Andy rubbing her arms, Jane holding her back, and Toby trying not to move a muscle in her face.

Finally, Andy couldn't help laughing. "What a mess!" she said. "We'll have to change our name from '407, Inc.' to The Walking Wounded."

Toby tried to chuckle with a straight face, and failed. "No more jokes, please," she begged.

Jane took a few steps, testing her back. "I think I'm going to be okay," she announced. "What I need is a hot shower, and then I'll be ready to work again."

"I guess I'll live, too," Toby said. "But today, the sunscreen goes on before I ever set foot outdoors."

"I don't think you have to worry about the sun today," Andy told her. "Take a look out the window."

Turning, the other two saw rain coming down at a steady pace outside. The sky was thick with a blanket of lead-colored clouds, and looked as if it would never be blue again.

"It's going to be one of those days where it never stops raining," Jane said.

"Not a great day for working in the yard," Andy said.

"I can't say I'm real disappointed." Toby was rubbing thick, white lotion onto her face. "Feels better already," she said. "So. If we aren't hauling branches and picking weeds today, what should we do?"

"There's plenty to choose from." Jane reached for her list and carefully sat back down on her bed to study it. Before they went off to shower, they'd decided to tackle two things that day — emptying out the sun porch and shampooing the upstairs rugs.

An hour later, Toby stood in one of the bedrooms, eyeing the rug shampooer. A short, bulky, square object with a long hose snaking out one end and two blue plastic domes on top, the machine reminded her a little of R2D2, and she wondered if it had his cute personality.

Randy, who had driven the shampooer from the rental store to the house, laughed at the look on Toby's face. "Don't worry — it won't bite," he said. "I'd stay to give you a hand, but I've got to get back to the farm."

"That's okay," Toby told him. "And thanks for helping us lug it up here."

After Randy left, Jane and Andy helped Toby load the machine with shampoo and then started to go back downstairs. At the door, Andy stopped. "Are you sure you can handle that thing?" she asked.

"Well, I guess it can't be any more stubborn than some of the horses I've trained," Toby said. "Don't worry if you hear me hollering. I'll just be giving it a piece of my mind."

Alone with the machine, Toby read over its instructions one more time. Then she plugged it in, took a tight hold on the hose, and flipped the switch.

* * *

Downstairs, Jane and Andy heard the whine from above and stopped at the door to the sun porch, listening.

"I don't hear any hollering," Andy said.

Jane nodded. "It sounds like she's got it tamed already. Come on, let's get started on this mess."

On a gray, rainy day, with no sunshine to brighten it up, the enclosed porch looked even more like a storeroom than it had before. But in Jane's imagination, it was already clean and airy, with lots of plants, and summery furniture in cool, soothing colors.

"I can just picture a comfortable chair right in that spot," she said, pointing to a corner where five dusty cardboard boxes were stacked. "A rattan chair, with pale green cushions. Or maybe a flowery print — they're very popular now. What do you think?" she asked Andy.

"Sounds good to me," Andy said, testing the weight of one of the boxes. "This weighs a ton! What's in here, anyway, bricks?" Peeling back a top corner, she shook her head in disbelief. "They *are* bricks!"

"You're kidding." Jane walked over and looked inside. Sure enough, the box was filled with bricks. "What on earth would anyone want with a box of bricks?"

"Let's hope it's just *a* box," Andy said, "not five boxes."

Jane tried to lift one end of the box and

failed. "Well, there's no question of moving these all at once," she said immediately. "We'll just have to take them out and carry a few at a time."

"Carry them where?" Andy asked.

"The garage." Jane took out some of the bricks and handed them to Andy. "I'm not about to lug bricks up to the attic or down to the basement," she said firmly. "That is definitely not part of the job."

It took four trips, but they finally had the bricks stacked neatly in one corner of the spacious garage. Unfortunately, the other four boxes also contained bricks.

"I don't believe it," Andy said, as they started in on the second box. "After this, those branches we carried yesterday would feel like feathers."

"Maybe they're planning to build a patio or a wall or something," Jane said, hefting another load. "Just be glad they didn't want us to do that, too."

As they trekked slowly from the sun porch through the living room, heading for the door in the kitchen that led into the garage, Jane suddenly stopped. "Do you hear that?"

"All I hear is my arms saying, 'give us a break!' " Andy joked.

"No, listen," Jane said. "That thumping sound. What is it?"

Cocking her head to one side, Andy listened. "Sounds like a" — her eyes widened as she realized that the sound was coming from up-stairs. — "like a bucking bronco!" she cried. "Come on!"

Dropping the bricks onto the living room's beautiful Oriental rug, the two girls raced into the hall and took the stairs two at a time. At the door to the bedroom, they came to a screeching halt, not sure what to do first.

In the middle of the bedroom was the rug shampooer, which had obviously gone berserk. Shuddering and whining, it actually lifted it-self a couple of inches off the ground, then crashed back down with a thump that shook the pictures on the walls.

To one side stood Toby. Gasping and try-ing to wipe her eyes, she was covered from head to toe in the foamy bluish shampoo that sprayed steadily from the hose she still held in her hand.

"The plug!" Andy shouted, and dashing through the spewing arc of soap, she pulled the plug from the outlet.

The shampooer thumped to the floor, then shuddered to a stop.

In the silence that followed, Toby finally let go of the hose, then lifted the end of her sweat shirt and wiped the suds from her face. Peering out of one puffy, reddened eye, she gave the machine a dirty look and drawled, "That thing is as ornery as a mule and twice as dumb."

Jane, who'd been speechless, opened her

mouth to ask a question, but instead she giggled. Clearing her throat, she tried to talk again, but giggled even louder. Andy's shoulders shook, she dropped the cord, clutched her stomach, and hooted with laughter. Toby looked from one to the other, her mouth curving into a grin. For a full three minutes, the roommates laughed until their sides ached and the tears ran down their cheeks.

Finally the laughter wound down, and Jane was able to talk. "I was going to ask why you didn't just turn the *ornery* thing off," she said, wiping her eyes.

"I couldn't see it!" Toby chuckled again and took a deep breath. "It didn't seem to be working right, and I thought maybe some rug fuzz was caught in the hose. So I lifted it up and just as I did, it went crazy! That first shot of shampoo hit me right in the eyes, and it surprised me so much, I forgot to let go of the hose."

"You should have seen yourself," Jane told her. "You were frozen to the spot, like some kind of weird, foamy creature."

"I can see the headline now," Andy joked. " 'The Suds Monster Strikes Again.' "

"Monster is right," Toby agreed. "Let's see if we can figure out what its problem is." Cautiously, she walked over to the shampooer and turned the switch off. Then the three of them cleaned out the dome where all the dirty water had accumulated, checked the hose for rug fuzz, added more shampoo, and got ready to turn it back on.

"Stand back, everybody!" Andy warned, her finger on the switch. "Three, two, one, blast off!"

As if it were exhausted, the machine whined weakly, sputtered once, and then died.

"Well," Toby said, privately relieved, "I guess we'll have to put the shampooing off. Randy's not coming back until two, and we can't get this thing to the store on our own."

Andy nodded. "So it's back to the bricks."

"Bricks?" Toby frowned. "I didn't know we were supposed to do any brickwork."

Jane was explaining about the boxes of bricks, when a voice outside shouted, "Yoo-hoo!"

"It's Penny," Andy said. "I'd recognize that yoo-hoo anywhere."

Running downstairs, they found Penny standing in the drenched front yard, wearing a bright yellow rain slicker and carrying a wicker basket.

"Have we got a story for you," Andy said as Penny came up the front steps.

"Then my timing's perfect," Penny said. "I was hoping you wouldn't mind if I wrote about this, but I didn't feel right coming empty-handed." She held up the basket. "In here I have turkey sandwiches, apples and grapes, a bottle of lemonade, and best of all — brownies."

The three roommates eyed the basket gratefully and ravenously. "I never even thought about lunch," Jane admitted. "We didn't bring any and there's nothing in the house but a couple of stale muffins."

"Perfect," Penny said again, pleased that she'd thought of it. "Let's have a picnic."

It was still raining, but the deck had a roof, so the girls ate out there, laughing and joking as they told Penny about the morning's disasters.

"This is a gold mine of stories," Penny said, her eyes twinkling. "You three are going to be famous once I get finished."

"Speaking of finishing." Jane took a sip of lemonade and a deep breath. "We really haven't done much, yet, and it's already one o'clock."

"Right." Toby started putting their trash into a paper bag. "We'd better get back to work, otherwise Penny won't have anything to write about."

"That reminds me," Penny said. "I brought one other thing — or rather two other things." Holding up her hands, she laughed. "These hands can work, believe it or not. Like I said, I've been feeling real lazy, so as long as I'm going to get famous writing about you, I thought I'd offer to help out. We talked about it before, but we were just joking then. This time, I mean it."

Andy and Toby laughed and thanked her, but Jane stiffened. This was a job, not a school project. She and Andy and Toby had been hired, not anyone else. Besides, after being told over and over how hard this job was going to be, Jane wanted to prove that they could do it by themselves.

"Thanks, Penny," she said, "but I'm not sure your helping is such a good idea."

"Why not?" Toby asked.

"I'm just not sure how Mr. Higgins would feel if he found out we let one of our friends help."

Andy laughed. "Why should he care?"

"Well, what if Penny broke something or goofed up?" Jane asked. "I'm not saying it's going to happen, I'm just wondering what if? We'd be responsible for it."

"I don't think Penny's chances of goofing up are any bigger than ours," Andy argued. "What do you think she'd do, anyway — throw the paint at the wall instead of brushing it on?"

"I didn't mean that," Jane said, "but I — "

"Seems to me," Toby interrupted, "that we'd be foolish to turn down any help we can get."

"Wait a minute, now," Penny broke in. "I was trying to be polite, but instead I started an argument. I certainly didn't mean to do that."

"This isn't an argument," Andy said. "It's a discussion. After we finish discussing, we'll decide."

"How do we do that?" Toby asked. "With a vote?"

Jane's face flushed pink with embarrassment. She hadn't meant to sound so bossy. "No, we don't have to vote," she said. "Penny, you're welcome to work as long and as hard as you want."

Everyone laughed at that, but none of them, not even Jane, had any idea of just how long and hard the work would turn out to be.

CHAPTER NINE

Dear Mother and Father,

Almost a week has gone by since we started working, and I apologize for not writing sooner. I know how eager you must be to hear about our job and how it's coming along. Well, it's coming along beautifully, I think. Of course, we still have two and a half weeks to go, and a lot of work to do, but I have no doubt that we'll finish and give the owners of the house exactly what they want. That brings me to the main reason for this letter:

Mother, I've scoured the town of Greenleaf for furniture and fabrics for the sun porch, and I'm afraid I've come up short. I need window coverings, and at least two small tables. I did find a nice rattan chair and a matching loveseat, and I bought them, but the cushions are completely worn out, and besides, the fabric was a hideous vinyl the color of mustard.

I was wondering if you would call that decorating company you used for our sun room — is the name Bay Design? — and ask them to forward me a catalogue and a price list. I just know they'll have exactly what I'm looking for. Thank you.

We are keeping very busy, but we make time for swimming and tennis, too. Meredith watches over us, but she does it without making us feel like we have a baby-sitter. Toby and Andy aren't here at the moment, but I know they'd send their regards if they knew I was writing to you.

Love,
Jane

Confident that she'd soon hear from her family's decorating firm, Jane sealed the letter. Then she took up the list of things she wanted to accomplish that morning and headed out of Baker House toward the post office.

As she walked — enjoying the first sunshine in three days — she was thinking that it was a good thing her parents hadn't decided to come visit this weekend, which they'd talked about doing. For one thing, the yard was finally drying out, and they planned to finish clearing it so it could be mowed. And for another, Jane knew her parents very well. They just weren't used to seeing their daughter doing hard, physical labor. They'd raised her to be a refined, well-mannered intellectual, and she had the feeling that the sight of her hauling branches, getting grime under fingernails, and sweating didn't fit in with their image of her. Her mother could understand decorating; it was the lugging of bricks and laundering of curtains that she'd have trouble with.

Actually, it was Penny who'd taken charge of the curtains. "I may have been raised to be a helpless southern belle," she'd joked, "but my mamma did teach me a few useful things, like how to recognize the quality stuff — and almost all of the drapes here are exactly that." While Toby and Andy and Jane had plodded from sun porch to garage with armloads of bricks, Penny had stripped the windows of their coverings, stuffed them in shopping bags, and carried them to the dry-cleaners. The rest, she announced, were washable. "Cold water and a hot iron" she said, "and they'll be as good as new."

Toby was right, Jane admitted to herself as she went into the post office, it would have been foolish to turn down Penny's offer to help.

Jane was fond of the Greenleaf post office; it had high ceilings with slowly revolving fans, smooth wooden counters, which smelled of lemon polish, and people working there who always recognized her and seemed glad to see her.

Today, though, with so many things on her mind, she didn't take time to appreciate its charms. After a quick hello to the woman behind the counter, Jane bought her stamps. Then she turned to leave and almost collided with Ms. Allardyce.

"Hello, Jane," the headmistress said pleasantly. "How is everything going at my friends' house?"

"Fine." Jane smiled cheerfully, but she couldn't help wishing that Ms. Allardyce didn't know the Browens. Being friends with them meant she'd take an extra-special interest in how "407, Inc." did its job. "Now that the yard is drying out, we're going to finish cleaning it." Which reminds me, Jane thought, I haven't found anyone to take away those branches, yet. "And next we'll paint the living room," she went on. "In fact, after I leave the post office, I'm going to the paint store to order supplies."

"Well, you certainly sound like you have your hands full." Ms. Allardyce tapped a stack of small envelopes she was holding. "These are the tea invitations," she said. "Are you still sure you'll be able to come?"

Jane, her mind busy trying to figure out how many brushes and rollers and cans of paint they'd need, didn't answer. She ought to go to the lumberyard, too, she thought, and soon. They hadn't done anything about those broken steps, yet.

"Jane?"

"What?" With a start, Jane came back to the present. "I'm sorry, Ms. Allardyce, what did you say?"

"I said I hope you'll still be able to come to the tea."

"Oh, yes," Jane said quickly, surprised that she'd completely forgotten about the tea. "We're looking forward to it."

"Good. Well, then," the headmistress said, "I can see that you're in a hurry, so I won't keep you."

Jane *was* in a hurry, but it wasn't only that she wanted to order the paint and get back to the house. It was as if something was at her back, pushing her all the time to walk a little faster, work a little harder, and rest a little less. In spite of what she'd written to her parents, she had this nagging fear that if she let up, even for a minute, things might fall apart. Not that she didn't trust Andy and Toby, but this job had been her idea. She'd had to talk them into it, and now she felt more responsible for it than they did.

The funny thing was, Jane didn't mind the way she felt. She liked being so independent. Smiling to herself, she thought even Andy would have to admit that she was doing a good job of organizing things.

All right, she thought, that's enough patting yourself on the back. Save that for when the job's finished. Still smiling, Jane picked up her pace and hurried on to the paint store.

A short while later, having ordered ten gallons of wall paint, five rollers and paint pans, three brushes, and six plastic drop cloths, Jane turned into the drive of the Browens' house. One hand still held her list of things to be done; in the other was a six-pack of soda, still icy-cold.

The pile of branches hidden around the first bend had grown by about three feet. Andy and Toby and Penny must have really been working hard, she thought, glad that she'd taken time to buy the soda. She walked on up the drive, expecting to see them somewhere in the yard, but the place seemed deserted. The front door and the garage door were both closed.

Frowning, Jane walked around the side of the house, and stopped. On the grass, (which was about a foot long, she noticed), were three hats. One was tan and belonged on a cowboy; that was obviously Toby's. Another was straw with a wide floppy brim and a long blue scarf attached to it; Penny looked like somebody in an old-fashioned painting when she tied it on her head. The third belonged to Andy, and as usual, it was very stylish — a purple baseball-type cap with a bright yellow plastic visor to keep the sun out of her eyes.

They must already be taking a break, Jane thought, impatiently checking her watch. It was only eleven; it wasn't time for lunch, yet. "Hello!" she called. "Where did everybody go?"

No answer.

Taking a deep breath, she shouted, "I brought cold drinks! Come and get it!"

"We can't!" Toby's voice finally shouted back. "You'll have to bring 'em here! We're on the deck, sort of!"

"What are you doing there?" Jane suddenly realized her voice had reached an undignified shriek, so she clamped her mouth shut and walked on until she came to the outside steps leading up to the deck.

At first, Jane couldn't understand what was wrong. Toby and Penny were at the top of the steps, brooms in their hands, and midway up sat Andy. Then, as she looked more closely, she saw that Andy wasn't just sitting there relaxing. She was there because she was stuck — the step below her had finally rotted through, and Andy's left leg was dangling between the treads.

"Are you all right?" Jane shrieked, forgetting about her dignity.

"I think so," Andy answered. "Nothing feels broken, anyway. I'm pretty sure it's just a bad scrape."

"How did it happen?" Jane asked.

"We decided to get out of the sun for a

while, so we came up here to sweep," Toby explained. "Penny and I made it just fine. But I guess after we'd climbed up, that old step just couldn't take anymore."

"We were just trying to decide how to get her loose," Penny said. "All the steps are a little shaky and we're afraid more of them might collapse."

Jane climbed over the two bottom steps, which were the only ones she had thought were broken, and tested the next one. Penny was right; it creaked, and it didn't feel sturdy at all. With a sinking feeling, she realized that most of the staircase was going to need rebuilding. But right now, the problem was how to get Andy free.

"Can you pry part of that wood away?" she asked.

"That's what I've been trying," Andy said. "Every time I move it, I can feel big fat splinters sliding into my leg."

The rest of them winced at the thought. Then Toby said, "If you could wrap your leg in something, maybe it wouldn't hurt so bad when you pull on the board."

Dropping her list and the cans of soda, Jane dashed around the house, snatched up Penny's sunhat, and ran back to the steps. With a twist of her wrist, she tore off the long cotton scarf.

"Perfect!" Penny nodded when she realized what Jane was up to. "Saved by the scarf!"

Searching on the ground, Jane found a small rock, tied one end of the scarf around it and tossed it up to Andy.

While the others watched, Andy worked the scarf between her leg and the cracked step, wrapping it around as well as she could. When she finished, she took a deep breath, then tugged at the step. "It's helping," she said, and tugged again. On the third tug, the splintered piece of wood came loose with a grating sound, and Andy's leg was free.

"Nobody breathe," Andy said, and then gingerly limped up, step by step.

Racing around to the front door, Jane let herself into the house and ran upstairs just as Andy made it safely onto the deck.

Silently, they all watched as Andy unwrapped the scarf from her leg, which did have an ugly-looking scrape and several splinters the size of toothpicks. "It looks worse than it feels," Andy told them.

"Can you walk?" Jane asked her anxiously.

"Sure," Andy said, getting to her feet. "I think dancing's out for a few days, but I'm fine. Really, Jane, you don't have to worry. This isn't a major catastrophe."

"I can't help it!" Jane said, still sounding much more upset than she needed to be. "You're lucky your leg's not broken. And we'd better get some medicine on it before it gets infected. I'll go see if there's anything in the medicine cabinet here."

After Jane left, Toby came right to the point. "What's eating her?"

Andy limped over to one of the picnic benches. "I'm not sure, but I think she's getting worried," she said, sitting down and sticking her leg out along the bench. "I think she's starting to get an idea of what a really big bite we're trying to chew."

"What about you?" Toby asked. "Are you getting worried?"

Andy laughed. "I've been worried from the beginning, haven't you?"

"I guess I have," Toby admitted. "But I haven't panicked yet."

"Well, Jane's about to," Andy said. "So maybe we'd better start to forget about knocking off early and going for a swim, or taking an hour and a half for lunch. Maybe we'd better just keep on chewing until this job is small enough to swallow."

"Fine with me," Toby said.

"I can still help, too," Penny reminded them. "And just in case nobody else listened to the weather report this morning — more rain is heading our way."

Toby and Andy glanced out over the yard and then at each other. "Looks like we'd better get cracking," Toby said, "or those weeds'll get so strong we'll never get rid of them."

Because of the rain, which came exactly as Penny and the weather report predicted, it took them three days instead of two to finish clearing the yard. But finally it was done. The branches and leaves were piled up and taken away (which cost much more than Jane had counted on), the weeds were pulled and the flowers could breathe again, and Toby, determined not to be outdone by another machine, had mowed the lawn so that it looked like a velvety green carpet.

During that time, Jane had also ordered the lumber for the steps, with Randy and Cary advising her on how much of what kind of wood to buy. Now there was a neat pile of freshly-cut lumber stacked next to the rotting staircase and covered with a plastic cloth. Every time Jane passed it, she felt good, until she remembered that it still had to be measured and sawed and nailed into place.

Jane also remembered that the rugs still hadn't been shampooed, the sun porch wasn't even half cleaned out, and the windows weren't washed. So on the day that the members of "407, Inc." gathered together to start painting the living room, she wasn't in the best of moods. That nagging fear was still inside her, and the more she tried to ignore it, the bigger it seemed to grow.

Andy wasn't her usual cheerful self that morning, either. The scrape on her leg was healing just fine, but it had been badly bruised, and it was very tender. Plus, Matthew was coming the next day. He could only stay one day, and she'd been planning to spend it all with him. Now, with the work piling up, she wasn't sure what to do. She really wanted to take the day off, but she didn't want to feel guilty about it. And she knew she would.

Toby had a problem, too. It wasn't giving up her afternoon rides at the Crowell farm or her tennis games with Dee. She missed them, but she could do without them for a while. Her problem was that she was coming down with a cold. Her throat was scratchy, her eyes were itchy, and her nose, which had been peeling on the outside, now felt like it was peeling on the inside. In Toby's opinion, there was almost nothing worse than a cold in the summertime.

Grumpy and edgy, the three roommates stood in the middle of the forest-green living room, staring at the cans of snow-white paint. The still uncleaned Oriental rug had been rolled up, and the furniture and floor had been covered with plastic drop cloths. Without a word, Jane took a screwdriver and started to pry one of the lids open.

"You forgot to shake it," Andy said quickly. "If you don't shake it, it's going to come out two different shades of white."

Jane stopped prying and sighed. "It's already halfway open," she said. "It's too late to shake it."

"Dough it's dot," Toby sniffed. "Just habber it dowd."

"Do what?" Jane asked.

Toby sneezed loudly, then wiped her nose on a tissue. "Habber it," she repeated.

"She means 'hammer,' " Andy translated. "Hammer the lid back down, then shake it."

The hammers were in the garage, and Jane didn't feel like going after one. Instead, she shoved the can to a corner of the room with her foot, picked up another one, and started shaking it vigorously. "Is that enough?" she asked after a minute.

"There's only one way to find out," Andy said. "Pour it into the pan."

"I thought you were the expert," Jane almost snapped. "That's why I asked."

"I'm not an expert," Andy retorted. "But I do know that paint has to be mixed. It's usually done at the store, with a machine. I'm surprised you didn't ask them to do it."

"I'm surprised you're telling me about it now," Jane shot back. "Especially when you could have mentioned it before."

"Wade a binnute," Toby said, and sneezed again. "By ears are doing weird things. I'be hearing busic."

For a moment, Jane and Andy didn't pay any attention to her, thinking that her cold was playing tricks on her. Then Andy lifted her head. "I hear it, too," she said. "And I don't have a cold."

By this time, Jane also heard the music. Putting down the can of paint, she stepped over the rolled-up rug and walked to one of the front windows.

Halfway down the drive, Jane saw Cary, Dee, Maggie, and Penny. Dressed in old jeans and ragged sweat shirts, they were marching toward the house with the kind of energy that she wished she still had. On his shoulder, Cary had propped a portable tape recorder, and its music was getting louder the closer they got to the house.

"What is it?" Andy asked impatiently.

"Freds," said Toby, who had joined Jane at the window. "Good freds."

"She means 'friends,'" Jane explained, waving back at Cary. She couldn't remember ever being so glad to see him. "It looks like we're going to have a party — a painting party."

"Good," Andy said, breaking into a smile. "A party is exactly what we need."

CHAPTER TEN

Laughing and talking all at once, the four good "freds" burst into the house, and the gloomy mood in the living room brightened up immediately, as if the sunshine had been brought inside, too.

"An amazing coincidence," Cary announced, setting his tape recorder on the floor. "We all have the day off, and when Penny told us she was coming here, we decided to tag along."

"Actually, she shamed us into it," Maggie said. "There Dee and I were, still in bed at nine-thirty. . . ."

"That sounds wonderful," Jane laughed. Staying in bed until nine-thirty was beginning to be a vague memory to her.

"It *was* wonderful," Dee grumbled good-naturedly. "But Penny made us feel like the two laziest people on earth, going on and on about how she was coming here to do some good, old-fashioned work."

"And the three of them recruited me on the way," Cary said. "There *I* was, out for a nice morning stroll, enjoying my freedom from The Greaf, when all of a sudden I found myself being ordered to report here on the double or risk being sneered at for the rest of my life."

"I absolutely deny everything," Penny protested with a laugh. "I simply pointed out what a great time we've been having at this lovely house, and how much fun they'd all be missing if they didn't come with me."

"She's right," Maggie admitted. "She tempted us."

"It's a lot easier than using brute force," Penny explained.

"So here we are," Dee said. "Ready to have a great time."

"Well, come on, what are we waiting for?" Cary turned the volume up on the tape and, spreading his arms wide, he leaped up like a cheerleader and shouted, "Let's have some fun!"

Fun was what had been missing for the past few days, but until the extra paint "crew" arrived, none of the roommates had realized it. Now, with Cary's music and jokes, Penny's endless supply of stories, Maggie's enthusiasm, and Dee's dry sense of humor, it was impossible not to cheer up and enjoy themselves.

For the moment at least, Jane was able to push that panicky feeling to the very back of her mind so that her confidence took over again and she was sure she'd pass her first job test with flying colors.

Andy, whose optimistic nature could never stay down for long, decided to take tomorrow off and not feel guilty about it. Matt was coming all that way on the train to see her and she wasn't about to make him sit around watching her work. The work would still be there the day after tomorrow, and they'd get it done. Somehow.

Only Toby stayed quiet, but it wasn't because she was still grumpy. Her cold seemed to be spreading, and though she didn't really feel sick, she discovered that her voice had almost disappeared. Since she wasn't a big talker anyway, no one, including her, noticed at first. But then Dee asked her a question, and when Toby opened her mouth to answer, only a raspy croak came out.

"What's the matter?" Dee asked. "Is something stuck in your throat?"

Shaking her head, Toby tried to speak again. Again, she croaked. "Oh, dough!" she managed to whisper.

"It's laryngitis," Andy said. "Toby, maybe you ought to go see Merry and get some medicine."

"I feel okay," Toby rasped, shaking her head again.

"Well, don't try to make any speeches," Cary joked.

"And drink plenty of hot tea with lots of honey in it," Penny added. "That's what my mamma always gives me when I have a cold, and it feels heavenly on a sore throat. That reminds me of a story," she went on, "about when I was a little girl and Mamma was the one with the cold. Does anybody want to hear it?"

"No!" everyone except Toby shouted teasingly, but Penny laughed and told them anyway. As usual, her story poked fun at herself, this time for pouring hot tea into her plastic kiddie cup and watching it melt onto the napkin as she proudly carried it on a tray in to her mother.

Even with all the talking and kidding, everyone worked steadily, first wiping the walls with damp cloths to get rid of dust, then beginning to roll on the first coat of white. Because there were seven painters instead of three, the room didn't seem as big as before, and by the time they broke for lunch in the early afternoon, the ceiling and two of the walls were done.

"We'll definitely get the first coat finished today," Jane said to Cary, pulling the paint-spattered scarf off her hair. "How many coats do you think it's going to take?"

Cary glanced around. The two painted walls were now a medium shade of green.

"Two more ought to do it," he said. Then he held out his hand, "Come on. Let's eat outside under a nice shady tree."

"There are plenty of those," Jane laughed, taking his hand. "We just finished raking all the leaves that fell off of them last autumn."

As Jane predicted, it didn't take them long to find a big shade tree. Hungry and a little tired from the painting, they sat down and ate ham and cheese sandwiches, not talking at all for a few minutes. Then Jane took a long swallow of iced tea and smiled at Cary.

"It's really great that you guys came over to help," she said. "I'm sure we could have done it by ourselves, but it's so much more fun with you here."

" 'Whistle while you work,' that's our motto." Leaning back against the tree, Cary smiled, too. "Actually, Penny said she thought the three of you were feeling slightly overwhelmed by how much you still have to do."

"She did?" Jane frowned. "Well, there is a lot more to do, naturally, but I don't think 'overwhelmed' is the right word for the way we feel. At least, not for the way *I* feel."

"Okay, if you're not overwhelmed, then what are you, underwhelmed?"

"Challenged," Jane said firmly, and then frowned again when Cary laughed.

"Hey, don't get mad," he said, reaching for an apple. "I believe you. And I think '407, Inc.'s' doing a great job so far. But I hardly ever see you at The Greaf or the pool anymore. In fact, I hardly ever see you at all," he went on. "And when I do see you, you look like you've spent the day building a house instead of just cleaning one."

" 'Just cleaning' a house can be tiring, too," Jane told him coolly. "Besides, it's a big responsibility."

Cary bit into the apple and shook his head. "I keep saying things the wrong way," he said. "I guess what I'm trying to say is take it easy. Don't let the pressure get to you because then nothing's fun anymore."

Jane scooted against the tree and leaned her head on Cary's shoulder. "You're right," she admitted. "I do take things too seriously sometimes. Especially myself."

"Hey, I've got it!" Cary straightened up, dislodging Jane. "You need a day off, too. Everybody needs a day off, right? I'm going to Boston to see my folks tomorrow, so why don't you come with me?" He laughed, pleased that he'd thought of it. "It'll be great. And I'll even make the ultimate sacrifice and go to the symphony with you, how's — " Cary broke off, confused by the look on Jane's face. "What's wrong? Did you wake up this morning deciding you hate classical music?"

"I love classical music," Jane said. "I always will. What's wrong is that I can't believe what you just said."

"What, that I'm going to Boston?" Now it

was Cary's turn to frown. "Come on, Jane, I'd love to stay here every day and help you out, but you were the one who insisted you could handle all this. Besides, my family's expecting me."

"I think it's wonderful that you're visiting your family. I'm surprised you haven't done it before this." Jane started rolling up their lunch bags, not looking at him. "And I certainly don't expect you to stay here and help out, even though it is a lot more fun."

"Well, then, what's the problem?" Cary asked, completely baffled.

"The problem is, I don't understand how you could suggest that I take time to go to Boston and hear the symphony," Jane told him, wadding up the paper bags into tight little balls. "You know how much work we have left — you never miss a chance to mention it. What are you trying to do, make it harder for us to finish than it already is?"

"Hey, wait a minute," Cary protested. "You're the one who keeps saying everything's under control."

"It *is* under control," Jane said.

"Oh, really? Well, you're not acting like it is," Cary told her. "You're acting like you're afraid everything's going to fall to pieces. And if a day or two in Boston will make everything fall to pieces, then it wasn't under control in the first place!"

Jane took a deep breath, but it didn't calm

her down. Not only was Cary trotting off to Boston as if he didn't have a care in the world, but he was suggesting that she do the same thing. He never thought she could do this job in the first place, and now that things were getting rough, he thought she should give in and give up. Too angry to speak, she leaped to her feet and ran into the house.

No one could quite figure it out, but after lunch, most of the fun seemed to have disappeared from the painting party. Cary was gone, but he'd left his tape recorder. Still, in spite of the music, the living room was gloomy again, and no amount of jokes or stories could brighten it up.

Andy's alarm was set for seven the next morning, but she was up before it went off. Matt's train arrived at eight-thirty, and even though her leg still bothered her and her arms were tired from stretching a paint roller three feet above her head, she wasn't about to miss it.

She took a quick shower, and when she came back into the room, she was surprised to see that Jane was wide awake. True, she was still in bed, but her eyes were open, and she was staring at the ceiling as if she were watching a fascinating movie.

"Hi," Andy whispered. "I didn't wake you, did I?"

"No." Jane blinked and turned on her side. "I've been awake for a couple of hours."

"You?" Andy laughed softly. "That's hard to believe."

"I know, but it's true."

Jane didn't bother to sound insulted and that troubled Andy. "Is something wrong?" she asked.

Jane's sheet rumpled as she shrugged her shoulders. "Yes," she admitted. "But I don't want to talk about it right now." Shifting around in the bed, she propped herself on one elbow and looked at Andy. "Why are you up? Are you going to do some exercises?"

"I should, but I'm not," Andy said, laughing again. "Matt's coming, remember? I'm going to meet his train."

"Oh, yes, I forgot." Rolling onto her back, Jane inspected the ceiling again. "I hope he's not too bored while he's here."

"Why should he be bored?"

"Oh, I guess he won't be," Jane said. "After all, he's helped us paint before. He'll understand."

"Understand what?" Andy had been toweling her hair, but now she stopped. "And what do you mean, he's helped us paint before?"

"I mean when we had to get the booths ready for the Almost Summer Carnival and the room ready for Princess Allegra when she visited the school," Jane said. "Matt worked with us then, so he shouldn't mind working with us now."

"Are you kidding?" Andy was rummaging

in her closet, trying to find a certain top. "You don't really think I'm going to put Matt to work, do you?"

"I didn't mean it like that," Jane said. "I just meant that since you'll be working, he'll probably want to join in, so he can be with you."

Andy stepped into her Hawaiian-print shorts and buttoned up an oversized yellow shirt. "Jane," she said, deciding to get it over with, "I'm not coming out to the house today."

Nothing moved but Jane's blue eyes, which swept quickly to Andy's face. "You mean you're taking the day off?"

"Yes, that's what I mean," Andy said. "Wouldn't you take the day off if you hadn't seen Cary for almost a month and he was coming to town?"

"I would if I had time," Jane said. "But Andy, we've got tons of work to do. How can you possibly think it's okay to spend a day doing nothing?"

Andy, who had been inspecting herself in the mirror, suddenly turned around. "I don't get it," she said. "You're the one who talked us into taking the job, saying it would be so easy. We can handle it, you said. Well, I've been handling it. I've been working as hard as anyone. And I'm not about to quit, but that's what you make me feel like I'm doing."

Jane sat up, throwing the sheet to the end of the bed. "I never said that you weren't

working hard," she replied. "I know you are.
What I'm saying is that you — that all three
of us — have to keep on working hard, or we'll
never get finished."

"Oh, great." Andy spun around and started
shoving things into her canvas shoulder bag.
"Now, when it's too late, you finally admit it."

"Admit what?" Jane asked.

"That we shouldn't have taken this job in
the first place. That it's too much for '407,
Inc.' to handle. That if Andy Cord takes one
rotten day off, then it's going to mean the
difference between success and failure."

"That's not what I'm saying at all," Jane
protested. "But you know how much is left to
do, and I just can't believe you're going to
leave it up to Toby and me."

"One day?" Andy asked, her voice rising.
"One day means I'm leaving it up to the two
of you?" She shook her head. "That's not fair.
You knew Matt was coming. I didn't keep it
a secret."

Jane had pulled on a fluffy white terrycloth
robe and now she was sitting on the edge of
the bed, staring at her feet. "First Cary, and
now you," she said.

"What does Cary have to do with this?"
Andy asked.

"He's going to Boston. He thought I
should take some time off and go with him,"
Jane told her. "I said it was a terrible idea
and we . . . we argued."

"Oh." Andy sat down on the edge of her bed. She didn't have to leave yet and besides, she didn't want to leave angry. "So that's what happened to the good times yesterday."

Jane nodded, but she was still so upset by everything that she missed the gentle joking in Andy's voice. "I still can't believe that he thought I could just pick up and leave."

"But Jane, if you really can't take any time off, and you don't think anyone else should either, then maybe things aren't under control," Andy suggested. "I mean, maybe we should wake Toby and talk about this. If things are that bad, then we've got to do something."

"Things are not that bad," Jane insisted, spacing her words out. "And we don't have to talk about anything. What we have to do is work."

Shaking her head, Andy stood up. "Yesterday, I told myself I wasn't going to feel guilty about spending the day with Matt," she said. "What I didn't know was that you'd try to make me feel guilty." Picking up her bag, she walked to the door and then stopped. "Well, I'm not going to let you do it," she said to Jane. "I'm going out, and I'm going to have a good time. Tomorrow, I'll be back working again, just as hard as anyone."

Jane didn't say anything.

"But I think you're wrong," Andy went on. "I think we're in trouble with this job. And since it was your idea to take it, I hope you at least find a little time to figure out how we're going to save it."

Jane still didn't answer, so Andy quietly left the room. After she'd gone, Jane sat there for a moment, her mind going over all the things they had left to do. Two more coats on the living room, an entire staircase to be built, four and a half rugs to be cleaned, all the dusting and polishing and vacuuming. Then there was the sun porch.

Rummaging on her desk, Jane pulled out the catalogue and price list that had arrived in yesterday afternoon's mail from Bay Design. The catalogue was sleek and impressive, and Jane could have furnished a dozen sun porches with the beautiful things in it.

But the price list was another story. Hoping the prices might have shrunk by magic during the night, Jane let her eyes rove over them. They were still high. Incredibly high. So high that it would take most of Jane's share of the money to afford them.

Sighing, Jane put the list back on her desk, and as she did, a small white envelope caught her eye. In it was the invitation to Ms. Allardyce's tea, which was being held in three days.

Looking at the invitation, Jane realized she couldn't possibly go, no matter how big an honor it was. There just wasn't time. Because in ten days, the Browens were coming back to Greenleaf.

We've got ten days, Jane thought, ten days to finish the job. And as her nagging little fear started to grow again, she admitted to herself, for the first time, that they might not be able to do it.

CHAPTER ELEVEN

After Jane went off to shower, Toby turned onto her back and opened her eyes. She'd been awake since before Andy had left the room, so she'd overheard most of the conversation. She had her own opinion about the situation, but she hadn't wanted to butt in, not in the morning anyway. Mornings were a time for keeping quiet, to Toby's way of thinking.

Besides, there was something wrong with her throat. Yesterday it had hurt, but not nearly as badly as it did today.

I can't be really sick, Toby thought. I never get sick. My throat's just dry, that's all it is. Sure she was right, Toby swallowed hard and instantly regretted it. Her throat was definitely sore, and one swallow made it feel like it had been sandpapered.

With a groan, Toby forced herself to sit up.

Her arms were heavy, and her head felt funny, too, like it was full of cotton.

All right, Toby told herself. You have a sore throat and a fuzzy head. It's just that blasted cold. It still doesn't mean you're sick. A shower and some hot tea and you'll be back on your feet in no time.

When Jane came in from her shower, Toby still wasn't on her feet. But she was sitting on the edge of her bed, and she'd managed to pull on the extra-large men's cotton shirt that she used for a summer robe.

"You slept late this morning," Jane commented, reaching with disgust for her paint-splattered jeans. "I hate to put these on, but I guess it wouldn't make sense to ruin a fresh pair. Oh, by the way," she said, trying to keep her voice light, "Andy's with Matt today. And Cary's gone to Boston. So with Maggie and Dee back at the library, it'll just be you and me. And maybe Penny."

"Jane," Toby whispered. "I heard you and Andy this morning."

"Oh." Jane frowned slightly, then pulled a yellow T-shirt over her head. "I already feel bad about that," she admitted to Toby. "As soon as I see her, I'm going to apologize. She was right — a day off's not going to make a bit of difference." What Jane didn't want to admit to Toby was how scared she was that nothing was going to make any difference.

That they were already too far behind to ever catch up. Admitting that to herself was bad enough; she wasn't ready to say it out loud yet. "I hear you still don't have your voice back," she went on quickly, "I wonder how long laryngitis lasts."

Gritting her teeth, Toby swallowed again. "Could you hand me a towel, please?" she asked.

"Sure." Jane rummaged in the basket of clean laundry next to Toby's bed, found a soft white towel, and held it out. "Here's — "

Jane broke off, staring at her roommate. She'd only glanced at her when she'd come in, but now she was really looking, and what she saw made her blue eyes widen with worry.

Toby's cheeks were flushed red, as if she'd put on blusher, which Jane knew she never used. Her lips were dry and her green eyes were bright and glassy.

"You're sick," Jane said immediately. "Toby, you look awful."

"Just a plain owd cowd," Toby croaked.

"Sure, and Max is just a plain 'owd' horse," Jane couldn't help teasing. "You look awful," she repeated, "and I'll bet you have a fever." Not bothering to find her shoes, she padded barefoot to the door. "You lie back down. I'm going to get Merry."

In three minutes, Jane was back with Meredith, whose dark hair was still damp from her own shower. She was wearing a long, green cotton robe and carrying a thermometer. Merry took one look at Toby and said, "I think the thermometer's just going to confirm the obvious. You've got a fever."

Toby just nodded, feeling too miserable to bother arguing anymore. Sticking the thermometer under her tongue, she lay back down in bed and closed her eyes.

"It's a good thing there's a doctor on call at the infirmary," Merry said to Jane. "As soon as we get her temperature, I'll walk over there with her."

"Will she have to stay there?" Jane asked.

"She can't," Merry said. "It's closed. The doctor's just seeing people there. The rest of the staff is gone for the summer." Looking at the worry on Jane's face, she smiled. "I'm sure it's nothing serious. It's probably an infection, like strep throat, and the doctor will give her something to knock it out. She'll probably only have to stay in bed for a day or two, and 407 will be fine for that."

Jane nodded, relieved, but Toby handed the thermometer back to Merry and whispered, "Day or two? Too much work."

Merry frowned as if she thought Toby must be delirious, but Jane knew what she was talking about. "She means we've got a lot of work to do at the house," she explained. To Toby she said, "Don't worry. The work will still be there when you're well. In fact," she went on, sounding much more cheerful than she felt, "I'll make sure to save some for you. How about shampooing the rugs — that was your favorite so far, wasn't it?"

Toby managed a grin and then said, "You go on, then. Don't worry about me."

Jane hesitated. It was true, she couldn't do anything for Toby that Merry couldn't, but she hated to leave her when she was so sick.

Toby waved a hand. "Go on," she said again. "See you later." She appreciated Jane's concern, but she didn't need two people waiting on her. One was bad enough. Toby hated being fussed over.

"I think Toby's right," Merry said. "If you've got work to do, then go ahead. And stop worrying. She's going to be fine."

"Well, all right," Jane said. "But I'll come back in a while, to see how you are."

After Jane left, Toby and Meredith got dressed and then headed for the infirmary. "I had something like this about a year ago," Merry said as they walked. "The doctor gave me some medicine. I'm not sure what it was, but it did the trick in about a day and a half."

"Good," Toby whispered. "Got to get back to work."

Merry smiled at her curiously. "Do you love the job that much, or is there another reason you're so anxious to get back to it?"

Toby held up two fingers, meaning there was another reason.

"Is it turning out to be more work than you thought it would be?" Merry asked.

Toby nodded. She hated to admit it, but it was true, and if they didn't do something fast, she was afraid they were going to make a mess of the whole thing.

Andy had been right, Toby thought. They shouldn't have listened to Jane when she talked them into the job. But it was too late for "I told you so's," and besides, they had to stick together, especially now. What they ought to do was come up with a new plan of attack. But Jane was being so all-fired stubborn and proud! She just couldn't admit that they were in trouble; she thought she could solve this whole thing by herself.

The problem is, Toby thought miserably as she trudged into the infirmary, with Andy and Cary mad, and me sick, Jane just *might* have to do it by herself for a while. And that'll be like using a shoelace to lasso a bull.

Determined not to let her argument with Jane ruin the day, Andy forced herself to put on a bright smile as she watched the train pull into the Greenleaf station. It was a beautiful morning, bright and clear and not too hot, and as Andy saw Matt step down onto the platform, her smile became genuine. Matt was a gentle, good-looking, soft-spoken guy, and she didn't have to fake being glad to see him.

"You look like a flower," Matt said, kissing her lightly. "Except for your leg," he added, noticing the bandage on it. "What happened?"

"On-the-job accident," Andy laughed. "Rotten steps can be hazardous to your health. Really, though, it's fine, or almost fine."

"Good." From under his arm, Matt pulled out a long, shiny, rolled-up piece of paper. "I got this for you at the ballet," he said, holding it out.

Taking off the rubber band, Andy unrolled the paper and saw that it was a poster. Done in shadowy grays and whites, it was a photograph of two dancers, a man and a woman, in a classical pose from *Swan Lake*.

"It's beautiful," she said. "Thanks, Matt. Boy, I wish I could have been there. I like Greenleaf, but it does get a little dull, especially in the summer."

"Dull?" Matt teased. "How could it be dull when you've got a full-time job?"

Andy laughed, but she didn't really want to talk about the job. If she talked about it, she might start feeling guilty, even though she'd told herself a dozen times that she didn't have any reason to. "Hey, I'll bet you're hungry," she said now. "Why don't we eat breakfast and talk about what we're going to do all day?"

"Good idea," Matt agreed. "That rumble you heard wasn't the train pulling out. It was my stomach."

Holding hands, the two of them walked down Greenleaf's main street, and out of habit, they wound up in a booth at The Greaf.

"That's funny," Matt commented after they'd given their orders to a waiter. "I thought Cary would be here. I wanted to tell him about this rock band I heard back home — they were good, but Ambulance had them beat by a mile."

"Cary would love to hear that," Andy told him. "He's always saying that Ambulance should go professional."

"Do you know where he is?" Matt asked. "Does he have the day off?"

"Sort of," Andy said. "He went to Boston to see his family."

"Oh, well, I'll tell him in the fall."

Their food came then, and as Andy took a bite of cantaloupe, she started to feel uncomfortable. Not with Matt, of course, it was impossible to feel uncomfortable with him. But when she realized that Cary wasn't there, she remembered that he and Jane had had an argument. And that reminded her of the argument *she'd* had with Jane only an hour ago. Shaking her head, she tried to put it out of her mind. This day is going to be fun, she told herself firmly.

"What's wrong?" Matt asked. "Isn't it ripe?"

"What?"

"The melon," he said, pointing. "You're not eating it."

"Oh." Putting her bright smile back on, Andy dug into the cantaloupe and started to take another bite. "Oh, who am I trying to fool?" she said, and put the spoon back down.

"I don't know," Matt joked. "Who?"

"Myself, that's who." In spite of the way she felt, Andy laughed. "Something's rotten in the state of Greenleaf," she said dramatically, "and it's not just a bunch of wooden steps."

"Sounds serious," Matt said, reaching for her hand. "Do you mind if I eat while you tell me about it?"

"Of course not!" Andy laughed again and picked up her spoon. "In fact, I'll eat with you. Now that I don't have to pretend to be bubbly and cheerful, I'm hungry again."

Eating at last, Andy spent the next half hour telling Matt about the job. She started with how Jane had insisted that they could do it, and then hadn't even bothered to see the house before she accepted it. "That was the first mistake," she said, starting in on an English muffin. "And then, when Penny volunteered to help, Jane got on her high horse and almost turned her down."

"Almost?" Matt said. "I take it she changed her mind."

"Toby and I changed it for her," Andy told him. "And it's a good thing we did. Now Cary's been helping sometimes, and Randy and Dee and Maggie, too. But if you want the truth, I don't think there are enough volunteers in the entire town of Greenleaf to help us get this job done on time."

Andy went on to describe everything, from the crazy rug shampooer to the broken staircase, to the living room that had to be painted at least two more times, since the owners wanted it white, not lime green. "And it isn't just things going wrong, either," she said. "It's just that the whole job is too much. For us, anyway. I mean, we can't build a staircase! We'd be kidding ourselves if we tried."

"And you think Jane's kidding herself?" Matt asked.

"Well, she keeps saying we can do it if we just keep working. If she had her way, we'd work around the clock." Andy took a deep breath and smiled at him. "I guess you can tell I'm pretty mad about it. In fact, Jane and I had a fight just before I met you at the train."

Matt finished his orange juice and laughed. "And I bet I can guess what that fight was about — taking time to see me, right?"

Andy nodded, embarrassed. She hadn't meant to get into this at all, and what had she done? Blabbed about it for thirty minutes straight. "Come on," she said, waving her hand in front of her face as if to push the whole thing out of her mind, "let's go for a walk and decide how to spend the rest of the day. That's what we were going to do in the first place, but I couldn't keep my mouth shut. Now I will, I promise. At least, I'll keep it shut about my big bad job."

As they walked, Andy kept up a steady stream of suggestions about how to spend the day. They could swim and have a picnic and then play tennis, even though neither one of them was a very good player. Or they could rent some bikes and go for a long ride, have a picnic and then swim. Or they could just hang out in the park all day, tossing a Frisbee and eating junk food. "Whatever you want to do," Andy said. "It's so good to be away from that house, that I'll be happy with anything."

Their walk had taken them onto the Canby Hall campus, and as they reached the wishing pond, they sat down in the soft grass on the bank.

"Everything sounds great," Matt told her. "But since my train leaves at seven-thirty, I guess we'd better not try to work it all in."

Andy smiled and looked into the pond. Pennies and dimes and even quarters lined the mossy bottom, and without meaning to, she found herself making a silent wish — a wish that she could go back and start this morning over.

She still thought Jane was being incredibly pig-headed, but Jane was also one of her two best friends. Best friends were allowed to be pig-headed once in a while, weren't they? Sure they were. And if Andy hadn't been so ready to get mad this morning, so ready to put all the blame on Jane, she would have been able to talk to Jane without attacking her, Then, together, they could have sat down and figured out what to do about the mess they were in.

Instead, they'd gotten mad at each other, and that just made the mess even bigger. So Andy stared at all the coins on the bottom of the pond, and wished there was a way to go back to the beginning of the day and be the kind of best friend Jane deserved.

"You know what?" Matt said, breaking into Andy's thoughts. "I just had an idea about what we should do today."

Andy turned to him, trying to smile brightly. "What?"

"I think we ought to go out to that house and see what's happening," he said. "I mean, I haven't heard about anything else since I got here." Standing up, he held out his hand, his dark eyes bright with laughter. "The least you can do is show me the place. Besides, I'd like to say hi to Jane and Toby while I'm here."

Grinning, Andy took his hand and stood up. "I didn't know you were a mind reader."

"I'm not," Matt laughed. "But right now your mind is pretty easy to read. You want to be at that house, helping get the job done."

"You're sure you don't mind?" Andy asked.

"Are you kidding? I came here to see you. I can see you just as well at your job as on the tennis court. Besides," Matt teased, "I'm a rotten tennis player and you're not much better."

Using the key that she'd triumphantly dangled in front of Andy and Toby just a few weeks before, Jane let herself into the Browens' house. The key didn't make her feel triumphant anymore; it made her feel tired and worried and weighed down with problems and responsibilities. It was just a plain, common house key; there was nothing unusual about it, but Jane couldn't help wishing she'd never set eyes on it.

In spite of her shower, Jane felt grungy, and as she trudged into the living room, she promised herself that after this was over, *if* it was ever over, she'd never put on an old pair of jeans again.

Her mood worsened as she thought of Toby and her flushed face and glassy eyes. Meredith had been so calm, so sure that there was nothing to worry about, but Jane couldn't help worrying anyway.

Jane had finally admitted to herself that she'd made a complete botch of this job, but if she admitted it to Andy, would it make any difference? Time was running out, and there was no way to grab it and turn back the clock.

Jane was too tired and upset to think of

any solution to the problem of how to do the job but to just keep doing it. Pouring paint into a pan, she picked up a clean roller and dipped it in.

As she painted, wondering how on earth anyone could have lived with a forest-green living room, she found herself missing yesterday's crowd. How could she have been so stupid not to welcome anyone who wanted to help them out? Not only did it get the job done faster, but it made getting the job done fun. Without the music and the jokes and the laughing, it was just a job. A hard job.

The pan was empty. Jane put down her roller and reached for the paint can. Just as she was about to tip it and let the thick white paint pour out, she stopped, listening.

The house wasn't completely silent. A noise she hadn't noticed before made her hold her breath, the paint can balanced in her hands.

Had they left a faucet on? The sound she heard was a steady drip, drip, drip. But it couldn't be just one faucet. There was a chorus of drips, like the forest after a rain.

Certain that they hadn't left on every faucet in the house, Jane set the paint can down. Just as she did, another sound came. This one wasn't as peaceful and steady as dripping water. It was loud and sudden, as if something very heavy and very wet had just crashed through the roof.

CHAPTER TWELVE

After the crash, the dripping kept on. Following the sound, Jane walked out of the living room, through the dining room and into the kitchen. The dripping was louder now. Feeling a little bit like a detective, Jane kept following the sound of the drips, which led her into the laundry room just off the kitchen. In the doorway, she stopped, staring in disbelief.

One wall of the laundry room was streaked with water, and more was steadily dripping onto it from above, streaming down in long rivulets and pooling onto the tile floor next to the washing machine. The washing machine, Jane noticed, had a new addition on top of it — a big chunk of wet, gray-white plaster.

On the ceiling, which was where the plaster belonged, there was a raggedy-edged hole, and as Jane looked up, more water gathered and started cascading down. She wasn't sure what had happened, but whatever it was, she knew it wasn't good.

Turning on her heel, she hurried out of the laundry room, back through the other rooms and into the front hall. She raced up the stairs, skidded around a corner and then stopped. There was another sound up here, one she hadn't heard downstairs. It sounded something like a shower running. Walking quickly along the upstairs hallway, Jane turned into the door of a bathroom and then stepped back, horrified.

The floor of the bathroom was covered with water, and the level had actually reached half an inch up the side of the tub. The shower wasn't running, and none of the faucets were on or even dripping, but the spraying sound kept going.

Stepping back into the flooded bathroom, Jane looked around, desperately trying to find the source of that sound so she could turn it off. But except for the water on the floor, everything else in the room seemed fine. It must be a pipe, Jane thought frantically. A pipe in the floor or the wall must have burst, and there's no way to get to it. And if somebody doesn't get to it fast, two rooms in this house are going to be completely ruined.

Jane's experience with plumbing was limited to turning on a faucet and watching the water come out, and she felt helpless standing there in her wet sneakers, listening to water spraying somewhere inside the walls. She wished she could just run away and let somebody else solve the problem. But she was the only one here, and besides, it was her job, so it was her problem. That's the way she'd wanted it, and it was up to her to do something about it.

Think! she told herself. You've got a brain, so use it. What do plumbers do when they come to fix something at Canby Hall? They always warn you that they're going to turn the water off. So there's a way to turn off the whole water supply of a house. All you have to do is find that faucet.

Trotting back down the stairs, Jane looked in the kitchen and laundry room, but didn't find it. Then she remembered the basement, and the minute she got down there, she saw it. On one of the walls was a pipe that seemed to be coming in from the outside, and right in the middle of it was a faucet. Jane twisted it as hard as she could, and keeping her fingers crossed that it was the right one, she dashed back up two flights of stairs to the bathroom.

Silence. The spraying sound had stopped, and Jane sighed with relief. At least she'd done something right today.

"I feel I should tell you, Ms. Barrett, that I'm getting a little concerned about your progress out at the house." John Higgins was a middle-aged man with bright, friendly eyes and a warm smile, but now, as Jane sat in his office, she noticed that his smile had more concern than warmth in it, and his eyes didn't seem quite so friendly.

After shutting the water off, Jane had started to clean up the bathroom, using a plastic bucket to scoop water into the tub. But after a few minutes, she realized that this wasn't just a matter of mopping up the water. A pipe was broken and would have to be repaired, and the ceiling in the laundry room would need replastering. She didn't know what that kind of work cost, but she had a feeling it was going to be a lot.

This was an emergency, she thought, not part of the original work they'd been hired to do. And that meant that Mr. Higgins would have to pay for it. So she'd left the cleanup for later, and headed straight for his office to tell him about it.

Mr. Higgins had seemed relieved to see her, and now she knew why — he was worried about the job they were doing and anxious to talk to her about it. "I got back yesterday," he told her now, "and so last night I took a drive over there, just to see how things were coming along." He shook his head. "You do realize, don't you, that my cousin and her family will be back in ten days?"

Boy, do I realize it! Jane thought, nodding

to him. She felt extremely uncomfortable, and in her white-speckled jeans and wet sneakers, she knew she must look completely different from the poised, confident girl he'd hired.

"Now, believe me, I'm not trying to tell you how to do your job," Mr. Higgins went on. "I don't know much about this kind of work, and I realize that things can look a mess one day and be completely finished the next. But you have to admit, you don't have much time left."

Jane nodded again, trying to think of something reassuring to say. Nothing came to mind.

"Why, the sun porch isn't even completely cleaned out yet, and that staircase won't get built in a day." Mr. Higgins took a deep breath and looked at her. "I took a chance when I hired you and your friends. I knew it was risky, but I did it anyway. Please don't make me regret my decision, Ms. Barrett."

"You won't, Mr. Higgins," Jane said finally. "I know it looks as though we're way behind schedule, but believe me, the job will get done." How it was going to get done, she wasn't sure yet. But it would. Mr. Higgins had trusted them, and Jane wasn't going to let him down. We'll do it, she thought. Somehow.

"Good." Mr. Higgins smiled, although Jane wasn't sure he was convinced. "Now, about that pipe," he said. "You call the plumbers and repair people and make the arrangements for them to do what has to be done. And have them send their bills to me. How does that sound?"

"That sounds fine, thank you," Jane told him, getting up to leave. "And Mr. Higgins, what I said about the job is true. We'll finish it, and we'll finish it on time."

"I'll only be a few minutes," Andy said to Matt as they walked into Baker House. Pointing to the empty lounge, which during the school year was usually crowded with visitors, she laughed. "I guess you won't have any trouble finding a place to sit."

Still smiling, Andy left him to take his pick of all the rather lumpy chairs, and started up the stairs to 407. As she climbed, she thought how lucky she was that Matt was so understanding. How many friends did she have who would travel all the way from Philadelphia to see her and then not mind if she went off to work instead of spending the day entertaining them?

Bursting into 407, Andy had already changed her shirt before she even noticed that Toby was on her bed, propped against the wall and sipping something from a mug.

"I don't believe you're still in bed!" Andy teased. "You must be sick."

"I am," Toby whispered. Pointing to a bottle of pills on the table next to her bed, she said, "but those little critters are going to make me well."

"Gosh, I'm sorry, I was just kidding," Andy said. "You look terrible. What's the matter with you?"

"Strep throat," Toby said. "Can you imagine? In the summertime, too." She took a sip of tea. "But the doctor says I'll be fine in a day or two." She pointed to a package on Andy's bed. "That came for you. I found it on my way back from the infirmary."

Andy looked at the brown paper-wrapped box and immediately knew what it was — a care package from her family. The Cord's care packages were famous in Baker House. Not only were they filled with delicious food, but they came at least once a month. If they can't hug me, Andy thought fondly, then they'll feed me. Turning back to Toby, she said, "I'll bet it's got cookies in it. Why don't I open it and you can have some with your tea?"

Toby shook her head. "Thanks. Not yet."

"Oh, right, your throat." Andy stepped out of her shorts and pulled on her jeans, which were paint-speckled just like Jane's.

"What are you doing?" Toby asked. "I thought Matt was here."

"He is. He's right downstairs waiting for me." Andy laughed. "I had a big case of the guilts for not working today. I didn't tell him that, but he guessed it anyway, and so now we're going over to the house."

Toby shook her head again. "One day won't make any difference. Not now."

"Yeah, I know that." Andy stopped moving around the room and sat on her bed. "I don't think Jane knows it, though."

"She knows. She just won't admit it." Sipping her tea, Toby shrugged. "'Course, I don't know what good it would do if she *did* admit it. It wouldn't get the work done."

"Now listen to me, Toby Houston." Andy stood up, her hands on her hips. "You just sound so pessimistic because you're sick. You know as well as I do that if the three of us stick together, we can do just about anything. And this job's no different. We'll figure something out." Reaching for a purple scarf, she tied it around her hair to protect it from paint. "I'm not going over to the house just to work, you know. I'm going to have a nice long talk with Jane. And if you didn't sound like you had a whole family of frogs in your throat, I'd make you come, too, so we could all come up with a new plan of attack."

Toby grinned. "That's what I was thinking this morning," she said. "That we need a new plan."

"And we'll have one," Andy said. "Just as soon as we put our heads together. I'll tell you what," she went on, "we'll wait until tonight to figure it out. That way you can be in on it. After all, we're going to need *all* our brain cells to solve this one."

When Andy left, Toby finished her tea and leaned back in bed. She was feeling better already. It could be the medicine, she thought, looking at the bottle. But she bet it wasn't *just* the medicine. Part of it was what Andy had said about the three of them. It was true, when they stuck together, they were hard to beat. Look at how they'd helped keep the school from closing that time the workers went on strike, and how they were always there for each other when things went wrong. We are a team, Toby thought, and if this team can't do it, then no team can.

From Mr. Higgins' office, Jane headed back to Baker House, just missing Andy and Matt. She had to call a plumber and someone to fix the ceiling, and the phone was off at the Browens' house. She could have used the pay phone at The Greaf, but she didn't have much change with her, and besides, going to the diner would remind her of Cary. She knew she had to think about Cary, but she didn't want to do it now, not when everything else was so up in the air.

First Jane checked on Toby in 407, and found her fast asleep. Good, she thought, seeing the medicine bottle, she's going to be okay. She looked longingly at the phone in their room. It would have been nice to stretch out on her bed and start dialing, but room phones were only for incoming calls. To call out, students had to use the phone in the hall.

A half hour later, that's where Meredith found Jane. The phone book was open at her feet, and she'd just set the receiver back with a slam that wasn't part of her proper upbringing.

"I don't believe it!" Jane said. "I just called four plumbers. Three of them weren't in and I had to leave messages on their answering machines. And the fourth one said he had all the jobs he could handle right now and wouldn't be able to do any more work for three months." She shook her head in amazement. "Three months! If a house had a bad enough plumbing problem, it could float away in three months."

Meredith couldn't help smiling, even though the situation was obviously serious. "I almost hate to ask," she said. "But why do you need a plumber?"

"I almost hate to tell you." Jane leaned back against the wall and sighed as if she'd been climbing the same hill for days and just realized she wasn't going to make it to the top. Then she told Merry about the burst pipe and the ruined ceiling, and her meeting with Mr. Higgins. "I knew he'd pay for it, of course," she said. "He's an honest man. But how am I ever going to get it fixed in time if

I can't get a plumber? And what would I tell Mr. Higgins?"

"Tell him the truth," Meredith suggested. "If he's honest, then he'll appreciate honesty from you. It certainly wouldn't be your fault if all the plumbers in Greenleaf are too busy."

"No, I guess not." Jane started to chew a fingernail, then caught herself and stopped. She bit her lip instead. "I guess I might as well finally admit it to someone besides myself," she said after a minute. "We're in trouble with this job. Never mind about the pipe and the ceiling, I'm not even sure we can finish the non-emergency stuff in time."

"What do Toby and Andy think?" Meredith asked.

"That they were crazy to let me talk them into taking it." Jane gave a little smile. "Andy's furious with me, and Toby probably would be, too, if she had the energy to get mad."

"Well, they might be mad," Meredith said, leaning against the wall next to Jane. "But I'd be really surprised if they were mad enough to just leave everything up to you. I've seen you three go through a lot together, and no one has ever jumped ship. Your friendship is too strong for that."

Jane smiled, a bigger smile this time. "You're right," she said. "But I do feel responsible for this. And I want to talk to them about it, so we can at least keep the friendship going." She picked up the telephone book and sighed again. "But first Andy and I had an argument, and then Toby got sick, and then the ceiling fell in! I feel like time's running out on everything, and if I don't find a plumber, I might just burn this book!"

"Please," Merry joked, "it's the only intact telephone book in the whole dorm. Listen," she went on, "I don't know exactly what the situation with the job is, but if there's anything I can do to help, you know I'll be glad to."

"Thanks, Merry," Jane said gratefully. "But the situation couldn't be much worse. I don't really know if another person with a paintbrush is going to make a difference."

"Well, you let me know." Meredith straightened up, and then snapped her fingers. "Of course!" she said. "I don't know why I didn't think of this earlier!"

"Think of what?"

"Bob Haskins!" Meredith laughed at the puzzled look on Jane's face. "You know Bob — he's one of Canby Hall's employees. 'Handyman Haskins,' he calls himself."

"Oh, that's right," Jane said. "He fixed the shower up here on the fourth floor that time it went crazy and scalded everybody. . . ." She stopped, her eyes brightening. "He can do plumbing?"

"You bet he can," Merry said. "He can do plaster work, too. And the best part is, he's working in my apartment right now, putting in new kitchen counters." She sounded relieved, happy that she'd found a way to help out. "I'll go talk to him. I know he'd be glad to take on an extra job, because he told me his son was starting college in the fall, and money's going to be tight."

"Oh, Merry, that would be great!" Jane said. "But what about your counters?"

"They can wait," Merry said, laughing again. "I don't do much cooking in the summer, and the old counters are good enough for my peanut butter sandwiches. You go on back to the house," she told Jane, "and if everything's okay with Bob, he'll be over this afternoon."

Jane kept reminding herself that only one problem had been solved — maybe — but as she headed back to the Browens' house, she couldn't help feeling that some of the weight had just been lifted from her shoulders. That nagging fear was still there, but its claws didn't feel as sharp as they had a few hours before.

As she walked up the drive, she noticed that the lawn needed mowing, again. How many more times would they have to do it before the Browens came home? Twice? And the weeds were back, trying to take over the flower beds. We've got a plumber, she thought, now what we need is a gardener. And a carpenter. And maybe a decorator.

Suddenly, she had an idea. She hadn't thought of it before because she'd been too stubborn to think of anything but her pride. She'd have to talk it over with Toby and Andy, of course. But if they agreed, then Jane thought she might have found a way for them to get to the top of that hill.

"Well, it's about time!" a voice called from the front porch. "I've been sitting here for an hour, ready to put my nose to the grindstone again, and I couldn't even get in the house. What did you do, sleep in?"

It was Penny, dressed in the same type of paint-spattered jeans that everyone else seemed to be wearing these days. Jane laughed. "I would give anything to sleep in," she said. "And once this job's over, I'm going to go to bed for twelve hours straight."

As they entered the house, Jane told Penny what had happened that morning.

"Now, that's a story that can't be improved upon," Penny said. "Are you sure you didn't make it up?"

"I wish I had," Jane said dryly. "Unfortunately, every word of it is true."

"Well, then, take me to the mops!"

Penny sounded as if the whole thing were a wonderful game, but Jane knew that without her, they wouldn't even be as far along as they were. "You've been great, Penny," she said, as they got the mops and walked upstairs.

"And you'll never have to worry about anyone thinking you're a helpless southern belle again."

Penny grinned. "Just call me a *tough* southern belle!"

While the two of them were mopping the bathroom floor, they heard footsteps downstairs. Then Andy's voice called out, "Hello! Is anybody here?"

"It looks like the whole crew is late today," Penny said jokingly.

"Andy wasn't supposed to be here," Jane said, putting down her mop. "Matt's in town for the day, and she was going to spend it with him."

"Hey! I've got a box of Cord's famous chocolate chunk cookies, straight from Chicago," Andy shouted. "Doesn't anybody want any?"

Did Matt miss the train? Jane wondered as she and Penny went downstairs. But when they were halfway down, she saw Matt, and besides him, Andy, dressed in her work clothes.

"I expected to find you painting away in the living room," Andy said.

"We would be, except for a slight emergency." Jane described what had happened and then said, "I don't get it. You two are supposed to be spending the day together."

"We are," Matt told her.

"I mean you're supposed to be spending it together having fun," Jane said.

"We are," Andy laughed. "We're spending it together here, having fun." Picking up a paint roller, she waved it in the air. "Come on, let me at that ugly green wall!" Smiling at Jane, she said, "I couldn't stay away. After all, we're in this together, right?"

"Right. Thanks, Andy." Jane was so grateful she couldn't think of anything else to say.

But Andy didn't seem to expect anything more. Her smile told Jane that their fight was a thing of the past. "I saw Toby, by the way," she said, "and I promised her that after Matt left, the three of us would have a big brainstorming session together so we can dig ourselves out of this hole."

"That's just what *I* was hoping we could do." Jane started back up the stairs and then stopped, pointing to Andy's care package. "You'd better save some of those cookies," she laughed. "If we're going to have a brainstorming session, then our brains will need plenty of fuel."

CHAPTER
THIRTEEN

At eight o'clock that night, after Andy had seen Matt off on the train, the three roommates of 407 settled back on their beds, ready to come up with their new plan of attack. On the floor, within easy reach, was the box of chocolate chunk cookies.

Reaching for one, Toby remarked, "Looks like somebody got to them already."

"A few somebodies," Andy said. "Matt and Jane and Penny and I just couldn't resist."

"Neither can I," Toby admitted, taking another. Having slept most of the day, she was feeling much better. Her fever was gone, and her throat no longer felt like a cactus plant had taken root in it.

Jane and Andy were in better spirits, too. The living room had received half its second coat of paint, the bath and laundry rooms were cleaned up, and Bob Haskins had come, located the broken pipe, and told them that fixing everything wouldn't be any trouble for him. That didn't solve all their problems, but it was a start. And what really made them feel better was that the three of them were all on the same side again.

"Well," Andy said, taking a sip of apple juice, "I guess we don't need to bother telling each other what's wrong. We already know that."

"Yep," Toby agreed. "It'd be a waste of time. Let's just figure out how to make it right."

Jane finished her second cookie and cleared her throat. "I was listening to Mr. Haskins today while he was looking for that pipe," she said. "He's a very friendly man, and he loves to talk. Like Merry said, his son's starting college in the fall, and it's going to cost a lot of money even with a scholarship."

"That's interesting." Andy looked puzzled. "But what's it got to do with us?"

Jane started to answer, but just then, there was a knock at the door, and Maggie looked in. "I heard a rumor," she said, her eyes roaming around the room. "A rumor about cookies."

Dee's blonde head appeared next to Maggie's. "I heard the rumor, too."

"I told them it wasn't a rumor." Penny, her dark hair frosted lightly with white paint, stuck *her* head around the door. "I told them I'd already eaten five, but they didn't believe me. They had to see for themselves."

Andy laughed and pointed to the box. "There they are — chocolate chunk cookies. Real, no rumors." She waved the three friends in. "Come on, there's plenty."

"What's going on, anyway?" Dee asked, as they settled down on the floor. "You guys look like you're having a super-serious meeting."

"We are," Toby said. "We're trying to figure out a way to get this job done."

"Time's running out," Andy explained, "and we can't keep up with it."

"I had a feeling things weren't going right," Dee said frankly, but she looked sympathetic.

Maggie's brown eyes were full of concern. "Maybe we can help you figure something out."

"I just wish I could do more," Penny said. "I'd be perfectly willing to work at night, you know. Maybe if we ate dinner there, and worked until sign-in time. Would that help?"

Jane smiled. "You three have been great," she told them, "but we can't ask you to do any more than you're already doing. In fact, I don't think *asking* for help is what we should do at all." She sat up straighter, leaning her back against the wall, and told them about Mr. Haskins. "And he told me that his son and some of his friends have been taking on odd jobs, trying to make all the money they can for college." Jane smiled again. "He also told me that his son is a very good carpenter."

"A carpenter?" Andy suddenly looked fascinated. "You mean wood, nails, saws, things like that?"

Jane nodded, her eyes sparkling, and Toby said, "I think what she means is a brand-new set of steps."

"That would be great!" Andy bounced up excitedly from her bed. "Do you think they'll do it?"

"Well, I'd have to talk to them, but Mr. Haskins seemed awfully positive about it," Jane said.

"Well, there's one problem solved," Dee commented.

"If they do odd jobs, maybe they could shampoo the rugs, too," Toby suggested. "That would leave us free to paint and mow and dust. We ought to be able to handle that."

"Good idea, but there's just one thing," Jane pointed out. "We'll have to pay them. And it's going to mean that we'll make less money than we thought. Maybe a lot less. How does everybody feel about that?"

It didn't take Andy and Toby long to decide how they felt about it. "The extra money would be nice to have," Toby said, "but I'd rather earn less and get the job done right."

"Me, too," Andy agreed. "Once when my folks were just getting started, trying to make as much money as they could, they took on too many catering jobs and wound up having to hire loads of extra people. But my father said it turned out to be worth the cost because it kept them their reputation."

"That's what I hoped you'd say," Jane told them. "I know we don't want to be in this business for the rest of our lives, but we do want people to trust us, no matter what the job is."

"P.A. would be proud," Dee teased. "You should tell her about this — she'll probably work it into her opening day speech about what makes a true Canby Hall girl."

"Oh, that reminds me," Jane said. "I think we're going to have to miss her tea."

"Now that's the best news I've heard in a long time," Toby grinned. "Getting dressed up for tea with Ms. Allardyce is just not my — "

"Cup of tea?" Andy finished, laughing. "It probably wouldn't be so bad, but I can live without it. But what about you, Jane? You love that kind of thing."

"Not as much as I'll love getting that house in shape," Jane told her, reaching for the care package. "Anyway, whatever she serves there couldn't possibly compare to Cord's famous chocolate chunk cookies."

Later, after the others had left and the three roommates were in bed, Andy's eyes flew open. "Jane," she whispered, "are you asleep?"

"Mm . . . sort of. What is it?"

"I just remembered," Andy said urgently.

"The sun porch. We didn't figure out what to do with it."

"Oh. Don't worry," Jane mumbled sleepily. "Trust me. I'll take care of that sun porch if it's the last thing I do."

The doctor had told Toby to take it easy for one more day, and even though she grumbled about being treated like an invalid, Jane and Andy wouldn't let her go to the house. "You just keep taking your medicine like a good patient," Andy said, "and tomorrow, maybe we'll let you mow the lawn."

Toby agreed reluctantly, and decided to spend some time writing a letter to Neal. He was never going to believe everything that had been happening. Or maybe he would, she thought, smiling to herself as she recalled some of the other scrapes the roommates had gotten into that Neal knew about.

The days of leisurely breakfasts at the diner were long gone, and as Jane and Andy hurried to the house, they ate buttered rolls and drank juice from Styrofoam cups. They didn't mind; after the night's brainstorming session, they knew they had a good chance to finish the job they'd been hired to do.

"What did you mean last night about the sun porch?" Andy asked, as they turned up the drive.

"I meant what I said," Jane told her. "I'll take care of it." In fact, Jane had already taken care of part of it, but she wanted it to be a surprise. "Look!" she said, pointing toward the house, "Mr. Haskins is already here. And somebody's with him."

Forgetting about the sun porch, Andy squinted. "It has to be his son," she said. "They look like twins."

Mr. Haskins *had* brought his son, whose name was Ron, and to Jane and Andy's relief, Ron said that he and two friends of his could start on the steps that very day.

While Andy painted in the living room, Jane spent part of the morning working things out with Ron and his friends, and then she went onto the sun porch and began clearing it out. The heavy things she left for when Andy could help, but she carted the light-weight boxes and broken pieces of chairs up to the attic herself, using a pull-down staircase in the upper hall.

She was coming down backward on it, holding on tightly because it wiggled, when all of a sudden it stopped wiggling. "Thanks," she said, thinking that Andy was steadying it, "I hold my breath every time I climb this thing."

"You're welcome," Cary said. "And you can breathe again. I've got it."

"Cary?" Jane hopped off the last two steps and faced him. "I thought you were in Boston."

"I was," he said. "Now I'm back."

"Oh." Jane looked at the floor and then at Cary. "How's your family?"

"Terrific, they didn't even make me wear a suit to dinner. Of course, we had dinner at home." Cary laughed. "So. How's your job?"

"Better than it was when you left," Jane said with a smile.

Both of them took a deep breath, and then started to speak at the same time.

"You first," Jane said.

"Okay. I wanted to say I'm sorry," Cary told her. "I thought about what you said — about how you had to stay and finish the job. And you were right. I should have known you couldn't leave, especially with the way things were going. You're the kind who sees something through to the end, and I like that." He smiled, his blue eyes very warm. "I was being real insensitive, but, cross my heart, it won't happen again."

Jane felt another weight roll off her back, and sighed with relief. "I wanted to apologize, too," she said. "Some of the things you said were true, especially the part about how the job was out of control. I knew it, but I didn't want to hear anyone else say it. I should have listened to you and everybody else." She laughed, glad that they both understood each other better. "Anyway," she went on, "did you notice that we've got some new people working?"

"I sure did," Cary said, taking her hand. "Where did those carpenters come from?"

" '407, Inc.' hired them, just this morning." Jane gave his hand a squeeze, and as they walked downstairs, she told him about the new plan. "I just hope it works."

"Sure it will," Cary said enthusiastically. "Hiring those guys was a great idea. The rest of us can take care of whatever's left."

"The rest of *us?*" Jane asked.

"Hey, you don't really think I'm going to stop volunteering, do you?" Cary shook his head and grinned. "No way. You already know I'm a brilliant musician, but you might not have noticed that I'm also a great painter."

"Oh, sure, I've noticed that you're a great painter — of walls, that is," Jane said teasingly. "How are you at climbing rickety attic ladders?"

Cary pretended to think about it. "On a scale of one to ten, I'd say I'm a seven."

"That's good enough." Jane laughed and pointed him toward an old chair on the sun porch. "Get going. And Cary?" she said.

"Yes?"

"Thank you."

Cary wasn't the only one to keep on volunteering. Penny came every morning, staying through the day, Randy showed up whenever he could get away from the farm, and Maggie and Dee came almost every day after working at the library. Jane and Andy and Toby tried to offer them money, but everyone was insulted.

"We're your friends," Maggie said. "We're not doing this for money."

Gradually, the work got done. Ron Haskins and his college friends built a beautiful staircase, solid and sturdy, and shampooed every rug in the house. His father mended the broken pipe, and re-plastered the laundry room ceiling so smoothly that no one could tell where the hole had been.

Every window in the house was washed and the clean curtains were hung back up, furniture was dusted and polished, the lawn was mowed twice more and weeds were once again pulled up by the roots. Three days before the Browens were to come back, the living room was finished, its dark green walls only a memory.

In the midst of everything else, the sun porch was completely emptied and its walls were given a fresh coat of white paint. With its newly cleaned windows, which wrapped around three sides, it was now a bright, sparkling, airy room. But, except for the cushionless rattan chair and loveseat, it was empty.

"It could be a great room," Andy said. She and Jane and Toby were standing in it, one day before the Browens were to be back. "But it's a little bare."

"It is now," Jane laughed. "But just wait.

It won't be long before it's the prettiest room in the house."

Just then, the doorbell rang, and when the three of them answered, a man was standing there. Behind him, in the driveway, was a truck with the name Bay Design, Boston, on its side.

"Oh, good," Jane said to the man. "You can start unloading. I'll show you where to put everything."

Speechless and confused, Toby and Andy stood by and watched as the two men from Bay Design brought in cushions covered in a soft, blue-gray-green material, a Chinese chest to be used for a coffee table, two smaller rattan and glass tables, two large plants in natural clay pots, and several hanging plants for the windows.

When they left, the sun porch was, as Jane had predicted, the prettiest room in the house.

"We could use a room like this at the ranch," Toby said. "It's like finding an oasis in a desert."

"It's so bright," Andy commented. "It makes you happy just being in it."

"That's what I was hoping for," Jane said, admiring the room. "If you two like it, then I know the Browens will."

"They'd be crazy not to," Toby said.

"It's perfect." Andy took another look at the room and then turned to Jane, her eyes questioning. "All right," she said, "tell us how you did it."

"I did it with a phone call," Jane said. "Come on, let's take a last tour of the house and make sure we didn't leave any rags or paintbrushes lying around."

"Wait a minute." Toby moved over to the doorway, so Jane couldn't get out. "When you two made me stay in the dorm that day I was sick, I got mighty bored after about an hour. So I was looking around for something to read, and I just happened to see the catalogue from that fancy Boston design company. Their prices are sky-high!" Her green eyes narrowed. "What did you do, discover oil on this property?"

Jane shook her head.

"Come on, Jane," Andy said. "You said you'd take care of the sun porch and you did. It's great. But how'd you do it?"

"All right." Jane went to one of the windows and looked out. "I couldn't find the right things here, and anyway, time was running out," she said, her back to Andy and Toby. "I feel like this whole thing was my fault in the first place. And I had to do something! I mean, I had to get the room ready, but I didn't want you guys to get stuck with it."

"Stuck with what?" Andy asked.

"The cost." Jane turned around and looked at them. "I had to get it done, so I used my share of the money and ordered what I needed."

Andy and Toby looked at each other, thinking about it. Then Andy said, "Well, it makes sense. Except . . ."

"Except why did you just use *your* money?" Toby finished, knowing that she and Andy had been thinking the same thing.

"I told you," Jane said. "I got us into this mess. And you guys were so great about working it all out. So I decided that the sun porch was a way to pay you back."

Simultaneously, her two roommates shook their heads. "Uh-uh," Toby said. "No way," Andy agreed.

"But — "

"No buts," Andy interrupted. "We're partners."

"Right," Toby said. "Equal partners. We divide up the cost of this room three ways?"

"What you did was terrific, Jane," Andy said. "But Toby's right. We're all in this together, remember?"

Jane nodded, too glad to speak for a minute. After all the worry and craziness and arguments, these two were still with her, two of the best friends she'd ever have. "Thanks," she said simply.

Andy patted her on the shoulder, and Toby grinned. "Now that we've got that settled," Toby said, "and now that the job is finally done, let's celebrate."

"Good idea," Andy said. "How much do we have to celebrate with?"

Jane dug into her purse and pulled out a pencil and a small notebook. She scribbled on it for a few minutes and then looked up. "Well, after splitting the cost of the sun porch three ways, I'm afraid the celebration can't be too elegant."

"I wasn't thinking of elegance anyway," Toby said. "What do we have left?"

With an apologetic look, Jane held the notebook out for them to see. The numbers written at the bottom of the page didn't take up much space. '407, Inc.' had made a profit, but just barely.

"It's not as much as we thought it would be," Jane said.

"No, but it could be less," Andy remarked cheerfully. "It's enough to help me buy some clothes for next year, or books and supplies. My family will be proud, just the same."

"Maybe we'd better forget the celebration," Jane suggested.

"Are you kidding?" Toby pointed to the notebook. "We might not be able to throw a party, but we can sure afford a good meal. And I'm starving. How about a big breakfast at The Greaf?"

As the three of them walked outside, Toby suddenly said, " 'Team 407.' That's what we should have called ourselves."

"That's good," Andy agreed. "That's what we are, a team."

" 'Team 407,' " Jane said thoughtfully. "I like it. Maybe next time. . . ."

Andy and Toby both stared at her, and Jane had to laugh. "Well, maybe not," she said, and still laughing, she linked arms with the other two.

Taking a last look at the house as they reached a curve in the drive, the three roommates realized they *were* rich — not in money, but in friendship.

When Andy and Jane visit Toby on her ranch in Texas, an unexpected romance blooms. Read The Girls of Canby Hall #27, THE ROOMMATE AND THE COWBOY.